Young Nurse Kate Murray is convinced that houseman Todd Morgan is just a rake with a string of
broken hearts behind him. Why then is she so disturbed when it seems he has abandoned his pursuit of
her?

*Books you will enjoy
in our Doctor–Nurse series*

CHAPTER ONE

KATE MURRAY disposed of her mask and hurried to change her apron for the third time that morning. She had just swabbed a great deal of blood and mud from a cut on a child's foot and managed to get some of it on herself, and Sister Carmichael was a stickler for clean aprons.

Kate loved working on Accident and Emergency, but the weeks in PTS had not really prepared her for the blood and the dirt and the smells, she thought wryly. Hartlake seemed to be regarded as the local surgery by many of the Londoners who lived in the rather dingy streets surrounding the famous teaching hospital and so they dealt with a lot of cases that might have been just as well served by the patient's own GPs.

The child with the badly cut foot, for instance. The canal that meandered along behind the backs of tall terraced houses, less than a mile from the hospital, was an irresistible temptation to adventurous small boys and there were some nasty pitfalls for bare feet in its murky depths.

It must have been painful, but the boy had stoically endured stitching, watching with interest and commenting with a practised eye on the workmanship of the doctor who plied needle and catgut so expertly. Shane was a well-known figure on A and E, being one of those accident-prone neighbourhood urchins who kept the department busy with minor cuts and sprains or the occasional fracture.

Golden summer days were the busiest, Kate had discovered. Children played in the streets and parks, in the canal and by the river, inviting all kinds of accidents. Pedestrians, lulled by the warm weather, seemed to take even more risks than usual when crossing roads. Motorists seemed to commit all the faults in the book. Hot and thirsty, people drank too much and fell over, cutting heads and breaking arms, or fell into argument and walked into A and E with broken noses or smashed teeth or cut lips. Wives were beaten and babies were battered, old ladies fainted and cardiac arrest seemed to become almost commonplace during the hot, glorious days. There was a constant stream of ambulances arriving or casualties being brought for treatment by car or taxi.

Whether or not the heatwave had anything to do with it, it had certainly been a very busy morning and Kate was glad to escape to the quiet of the juniors' room. There, she could not hear the swish of rubber wheels as trolleys were trundled to and fro, or the clatter of instruments as casualty officers sutured or probed or dressed the constant flow of patients. For a few moments she would not be required to wheel a patient to X-ray or ward, soothe a fractious child or reassure an anxious mother, remove a dirty bandage from a festering finger or clean blood and grime from cut face or knee, lay up a trolley with swabs and instruments and bandage packs or hurry for fresh supplies of syringes and ampules or be sent to the Path Lab with blood sample or specimen. She could relax.

She put on a clean apron and pinned the tiny white cap with its one blue stripe denoting the first-year nurse more securely into place. Her silky blonde hair had recently been cut short in the latest fashion and one wing insisted on falling forward over her brow. It was rapidly becoming the bane of her life, she thought ruefully, regretting the pale, shoulder-length tumble of waves and curls that she had sacrificed.

She had soon found that there was little time to spend on face and hair between falling out of bed and reporting to Sister Tutor for lectures in anatomy, physiology and hygiene or practical work in readiness for the wards. It had seemed sensible to cut her hair short so that she only needed to run a brush through it.

It was that delicate shade of ash-blonde that few people believed to be her natural colouring. She had the almost translucent skin of the true blonde, wide grey eyes fringed with long dark lashes, small and slender nose and the kind of mouth that magazine stories liked to describe as kissable. She had a particularly enchanting smile, too. Kate was more than merely pretty. She was beautiful. The purity of bone structure and the cool delicacy of colouring ensured that her looks caught the eye at the hospital that had more than its fair share of pretty nurses.

Young men who came into A and E with broken bones for X-ray and setting or deep cuts for suturing almost forgot their woes in the pleasure of looking at the lovely face and slender figure in the blue check frock with its puffed sleeves that was the traditional uniform of a Hartlake first-year nurse. She also attracted a great deal of attention from the susceptible young doctors and medical students who welcomed each new intake of nurses with delight and openly amorous intent.

Kate was too used to her looks to rate them very highly. Being shy and rather modest, she was not very encouraging towards most of the young men who pursued her and she was anxious not to be labelled as a flirt. Matron disapproved of romantic relationships between members of the staff. Flirtation might be rife at Hartlake, but nurses soon learned to be discreet. For it was always the girl who was hauled before Matron for a scold or a warning, or even dismissal in some cases.

Kate's position was particularly awkward, she felt. For her father was a consultant who took a weekly clinic at Hartlake—and her mother had been a ward sister at the hospital some twenty years before. In the circumstances, it was probably natural that Matron should keep a watchful eye on a girl she had known in the cradle and who might too easily fall prey to one of the rakish young doctors who laid siege to her nurses instead of concentrating on their work. Perhaps that was the reason why Kate had been sent to Accident and Emergency from the Preliminary Training School instead of a ward like the rest of her set. Perhaps Matron had believed that in such a busy department, no one would have time to waste in flirtation.

In fact, several doctors had found time to lay siege to Kate. Some because any first-year nurse was fair game—in many cases, they were straight from school, too innocent or too inexperienced to realise the dangers in flattery and flirtation, easily impressed by a certain glamour that young men seemed to acquire with the donning of a white coat. But most of them because Kate's shy, sweet smile and very expressive eyes and unconsciously alluring resistance to their persuasions had captivated them swiftly.

Kate had grown up in a world of medicine and white coats. She was not bewitched by the glamour that attached to training and working in a famous London hospital and she was not over-awed by her surroundings or her seniors. She had been better prepared than most of her set for the long hours and the hard work and the mental, physical and emotional demands of training. She had set her heart on being a state registered nurse and she did not mean to be deflected from achieving that ambition by falling foolishly in love.

Matron would have been glad to make an exception in her case to the rule that first-year nurses must live in the Nurses' Home, irreverently dubbed the Nunnery by medical students, but Kate had chosen to share a flat there with three other girls. She enjoyed the independence and the company, and living in had given her an insight into the tangled love lives of some of the girls, but she had soon decided to steer clear of such emotional entanglements herself.

She liked men, of course. She liked to dance and go to parties and there were plenty of opportunities for a social life despite long hours of work and the need to study. But as soon as an escort seemed to be growing too fond of her, or she found herself thinking about him instead of her work, Kate was careful to cool the relationship.

Sister Carmichael opened the door of the juniors' room. Kate hastily turned from the mirror and the final adjustment to the cap that slipped too easily on her soft, pale hair.

'Now come along, Nurse! I've a patient for Theatres and another one to go to X-ray and we're running short of sterile surgical packs. There's no time to dawdle this morning!'

'Yes, Sister. Sorry, Sister.'

Kate knew that tone of voice and already knew better than to ignore it. Instant obedience was one of the first things that a nurse had to learn. She must not hesitate or question but simply do as she was told. Sister Tutor had stressed that a moment's hesitation in obeying an instruction could cost a patient's life in an emergency. Like most juniors, Kate had learned that it was also likely to bring a stinging rebuke or the threat of Matron's Report from a rushed and overworked sister or staff nurse.

The patient that she took to X-ray was a woman of eighty-one, very frail and shaken by a bad fall. She had been balanced precariously on a rickety kitchen chair to take down some net curtains for washing when the chair slipped. She had injured her knee and bruised her head and hip. She lived alone, but her cries had alerted a kindly neighbour who had called an ambulance. The old lady was badly shocked and in pain, but little could be done to alleviate her distress until the radiographer had done her work and the doctors knew what damage had been done to her swollen knee and whether surgery was necessary.

She was crying silently, tears streaming down the wrinkled cheeks, and clinging painfully to Kate's hand as a porter wheeled her on a trolley across Main Hall. Kate held the folder that contained the little information they had managed to extract from the patient and the neighbour who had accompanied her to hospital.

Main Hall was a bustling hive of activity, efficiently presided over by the head porter who had been at Hartlake for thirty years and was very much a part of its long tradition. However busy he might be, nothing seemed to escape Jimmy's notice.

Now, he smiled and winked at Kate and said something to the tall man in the white coat who stood by the reception desk, busily writing on a pad. The doctor glanced up and looked directly into Kate's grey eyes. At first indifferent, his expression abruptly sharpened to unmistakable interest.

Caught looking at him, Kate glanced away, annoyed by the slight quickening of her pulses and the warmth that she felt in her cheeks. She knew all about Todd Morgan and his fickle attentions and she had not the slightest desire to attract his interest, she told herself firmly.

Walking with the trolley as it turned the corner and headed for the X-ray department, Kate wondered idly what Jimmy had said to the good-looking houseman whose main occupation in life seemed to be the pursuit of women rather than medicine. Tall, dark-haired and with incredibly blue eyes that seemed to have the power to compel a woman's liking and affection and compliance, he was much too attractive for any woman's peace of mind—or his own good, Kate decided with a faint stirring of disapproval for a man who had been involved with too many girls, if the grapevine was to be believed.

She had seen admiration and something more in that quick and very direct glance, but she doubted that anything would come of such a fleeting interest. It seemed that he did not bother with the first-years. No doubt they were too young and inexperienced for someone as reputedly sensual as Todd Morgan. She did not think that sweet and trusting innocents could be much to his taste. He had a reputation for being a Casanova who took and used and discarded women with little thought for anything but his own satisfaction. In fact, he was obviously the kind of man that any self-respecting girl would be wise to avoid!

Kate wondered ruefully why the most exciting men were always too dangerous to be trusted while the safe and reliable types were usually lacking in both looks and glamour. She supposed it was Todd Morgan's good looks and reputed charm and that air of rakishness that made him so exciting.

Waiting while the radiographer took several plates of X-rays of old Mrs Jennings, Kate allowed herself to day-dream, rather foolishly. She did not really want to know Todd Morgan or his kind, of course. She was not really stirred by his brand of good looks. She had come to Hartlake to nurse and not to be a doctor's delight like some of the juniors, and he was the type who apparently made the most of the opportunities amongst Hartlake's young and often pretty and sometimes too impressionable nurses.

Kate had seen him often and heard much about him. But she had never actually spoken to him or met him and she doubted if he had known of her existence until ten minutes before—and she only had Jimmy to thank for that momentary flicker of interest. Perhaps the head porter had mentioned that she was the daughter of Sir Terence Murray.

Jimmy had a bubbling sense of humour, a warm friendliness and a fund of sympathetic humanity that endeared him to all. Kate had known him all her life and discovered at an early age that he was an almost legendary figure and one of the mainstays of Hartlake tradition. He was also the main root of the hospital grapevine, she suspected. An incurable romantic, he smiled on minor flirtations among the staff and could not be more delighted if one of them developed into a full-scale affair with a happy ending. It was said that he always knew when romance was in the air and was seldom wrong in predicting if it would end in happiness or heartache. But that was the kind of legend about himself that the big man enjoyed and encouraged.

It was not likely that someone as lovely as the grown-up Kate could escape his notice, even if he had not immediately recognised her in the uniform of a first-year nurse. On her first day, Kate had crossed Main Hall with a group of nurses as green as herself. Having a quick eye for a pretty face and an unerring instinct for knowing when a new nurse would stand out from the others in her set, Jimmy had beckoned her to the reception desk and asked her name.

He had nodded sagely on hearing it. 'Of course it is!' he had declared, twinkling. 'Little Kate Murray! The image of your mum, too! I remember the day she brought you here as a baby to show you off to her friends. Seen you grow up, I have—and grown prettier every year! Glad to see you following in your mum's footsteps. You'll make Nurse of the Year with your background, I shouldn't wonder!'

Kate had smiled shyly and begged him not to tell everyone of her relationship to a famous and very successful specialist. She wanted to make good on her own merits and Murray was a common enough name. Jimmy had faithfully promised to keep her secret and she had hurried to catch up with her new friends, thinking wryly that there were too many people who wouldn't forgive her if she did not live up to the promise of being the daughter of Sir Terence and a former ward sister!

It was a daunting challenge and sometimes she wondered if she should have applied to train at another hospital. But Hartlake nurses were famous all over the world and she had grown up with stories about the hospital's traditions and legends. It seemed that there was really only one teaching hospital worthy of the name, if her parents were to be believed, and Kate could not recall a time when she had not wanted to be a Hartlake nurse.

She doubted that Jimmy had kept his promise, for it seemed that most people knew that Sir Terence was her father. He was a brilliant and highly-respected member of his profession and Kate was very proud of him. She wanted him to be proud of her, too. She doubted if she could make Nurse of the Year, for that would require rather longer hours of study and devotion to textbooks than she might always be inclined to give. Young and pretty and with plenty of friends, she liked to enjoy herself. But she meant to do her best to get good marks for her theory and good reports for her practical work on A and E and the wards.

Which meant that it would be most unwise to know a man like Todd Morgan—or even to dream about him, she told herself sternly.

But he really was very attractive . . .

Tall, broad-shouldered and narrow-hipped, lean and lithe and muscular. Dark hair curled crisply on the nape of his neck and waved deeply from the temples. His eyes were particularly striking, very blue and deep-set and with a certain glow in their depths when he looked at a woman that made the heartbeat quicken just a fraction. The warm, rather sensual mouth could quirk in a swift and disarming smile that most women seemed to find devastating.

His good-looking face had the kind of complexion that hinted at summer tan even in winter. A touch of the dago, someone had said in Kate's hearing, slightly contemptuous. A touch of the Celt was more likely, she thought. That black hair and those very blue eyes and the hint of hot-blooded sensuality in his attitude to any pretty girl who crossed his path hinted at Welsh or Irish forebears. So did his rather unusual name. But Todd suited him—strong, masculine and direct like the man himself.

A very attractive man, but a dangerous one, Kate felt, remembering the stir of her senses as their eyes met. Delicious and rather disturbing and certainly not to be encouraged unless she wanted to be one more in a long list of his sexual conquests.

It was unlikely that he had given her another thought. It was really rather foolish to be dreaming about the good looks and fatal fascination of a man who was said to have been the downfall of too many girls.

She was jerked back to reality as Mrs Jennings vomited and choked and clutched at her heart with a gasping little cry. Suddenly her face was ashen as she fought for breath. Kate moved swiftly to turn the patient's head to one side. Without conscious thought, her fingers sought a pulse in the old lady's wrist—and failed to find it! She turned anguished eyes to the radiographer who took in the situation at a glance.

'Cardiac arrest! Get help!' Even as she spoke, the girl had the heel of one hand with the weight of the other over it pressed on Mrs Jenning's chest and was rhythmically squeezing and compressing the heart against the vertebral column.

Kate ran. She clutched at the first white coat she saw in the corridor. 'Please come—emergency! Cardiac arrest!' she blurted, not noticing that it was Todd Morgan until he turned. She was much too concerned for the patient who had seemed even to her inexperienced eye to be close to death.

'Where?' He was already running.

'Room 3, X-ray . . .'

'Dial 1!' he threw at her over his shoulder and Kate sped to the nearest telephone, realising that it should have been her first reaction to alert the cardiac arrest team. By the time she joined them, Todd Morgan had taken over manual respiration and the radiographer had the oxygen bag and mask and was forcing air into the old lady's lungs.

Kate hovered helplessly, feeling inadequate and realising how much she had to learn. Almost immediately, the room was filled with people as the cardiac arrest team arrived, knowing exactly what to do. Kate was pushed brusquely to one side. Someone injected cortisone to stimulate the heart and strengthen its contractions. An anaesthetist positioned an endotracheal tube down the windpipe and attached it to the oxygen. Todd Morgan was bent over the patient, still forcing the oxygen and the drugs into the coronary circulation. A staff nurse was busily drawing other drugs into syringes, labelling them and placing them side by side on a trolley in case of need. Another nurse attached an oscilloscope to the patient so that the electrical activity of the heart could be monitored.

Within a few more minutes, Mrs Jennings showed signs of returning consciousness and Kate felt her own heart lift with relief. She knew she would have felt responsible in some way if the old lady had died. She slipped from the room to struggle with threatening tears. No longer needed, Todd Morgan followed her into the corridor, chest still heaving and beads of sweat on his brow. Glancing at Kate, he was abruptly aware of her now that he had time to recognise her with the emergency behind him. Interest quickened in his very blue eyes.

'You saved her life!' she said impulsively, forgetting that first-years did not address senior doctors except in the course of their work.

He shrugged, smiled. 'Combined efforts,' he said lightly. The personal radio in his breast pocket began to 'bleep' and he winked at her in friendly fashion before striding to the telephone.

Kate looked after him, marvelling at his casual manner. But no doubt he was used to sudden crises. She felt that it had been a very traumatic experience!

Mrs Jennings was whisked off to Intensive Care, the necessary surgery for a shattered patella postponed while she remained under careful observation, and Kate went back to A and E. As she crossed Main Hall, Jimmy beckoned. Slightly suspicious of his broad smile and a meaningful twinkle in his eye, she went over to the big desk.

'Note for you, Nurse.' He handed her an envelope.

Kate blushed fierily. Suddenly sure that the note came from Todd Morgan, she thrust it into the deep pocket of her uniform frock without even glancing at the inscription. She told herself firmly that she wouldn't bother to read the note. She wasn't interested in anything he might say, or write!

She hurried to report to Sister Carmichael who must be wondering at her long absence. Thrusting through the swing doors into A and E, she collided with Todd Morgan's tall frame. He steadied her with both hands on her slender waist. 'You're in a hurry,' he said lightly. 'Not another cardiac arrest?'

Kate didn't smile. She wondered that he could be so flippant and she was furious with herself for flying such bright banners in her cheeks—and furious with him for rocking her senses with his touch. 'Not funny!' she snapped.

He looked down at her steadily. 'Laugh when you can or you'll be torn to pieces in this place,' he said quietly.

Kate didn't like the way her heart fluttered as she met his eyes. 'I'm busy,' she said abruptly.

'Aren't we all?' His tone was wry.

'Then don't waste time writing notes to me and I won't waste time in reading them,' she said quickly. Head high, she brushed past him.

Todd stood motionless for a moment, a slightly arrested expression in his narrowed eyes. He had noted that she was a very pretty girl, but with his mind on other matters he had dismissed the slender blonde junior. Now, he was jolted into a renewed awareness of her.

Since his early days as a medical student, it had been his policy to steer clear of first-year nurses. They were usually very young and rather naive and they took everything too seriously—and some of them were more interested in marriage than medicine. He preferred to enjoy a succession of light affairs with girls who were older and wiser and experienced in the game of flirtation.

He knew he was regarded as a rake who had left a string of broken hearts behind him. It was an exaggeration. It was true that there had been plenty of girls, but none had been encouraged to cherish false illusions about his feelings or false hope for the future. He did not have marriage in mind and said so frankly at the start of an affair.

But suddenly Todd was tempted to forget his own ruling about the first-years. A brief encounter with a girl whose name he did not even know had stirred his jaded senses. He liked the cool and delicate beauty of face and figure. He fancied he could span that little waist easily with two hands. The small tilting breasts were a delight and a challenge to a man of his sensuality. The pale hair, the delightful skin, the wide grey eyes with their militant sparkle all enchanted him.

It was a long time since he had known desire at first sight . . .

CHAPTER TWO

A AND E continued to be busy. Kate might be a very junior nurse, but she was expected to cope with sights and sounds that lesser mortals would abhor.

Sent to clean up the victim of a road accident, she gingerly and very gently swabbed blood and vomit from face and chest and abdomen, her eyes smiling reassurance over her mask. Her patient was conscious, but very confused after an injection that one of the casualty officers had given him to ease the pain of a broken leg. Suddenly he clutched at her hand and turned an ominous colour, then vomited again, all over her reasonably clean apron.

It was only when she found a moment to change that she remembered Todd Morgan's note. She drew it from her pocket. Then, telling herself that it was only curiosity, she opened the envelope. It would be rather interesting to find how he phrased his first overtures to a girl.

She stared, astonished and dismayed, at the brief message in her father's neat hand. Leaping to conclusions, she had made a fool of herself—and she did not much like the feeling!

Later, she sat in the hospital garden beneath the bronze statue of Sir Henry Hartlake, founder of the hospital, and read her father's note again.

'*Dearest Kate, it's too long since we've seen each other,*' he had written, gently chiding her for neglect. She hadn't been home in ten days, although she'd talked to her parents on the telephone. *'Tear yourself away from those young doctors and take pity on a lonely man. Have dinner with me this evening . . .'*

Kate smiled affectionately. She and her father were very close. Her mother would be out that evening, she knew, attending a committee meeting of the Friends of Hartlake Hospital to discuss various fund-raising events for Founder's Week. Coinciding with the third week in June and often blessed with excellent weather, it was the most important week of the hospital year and always ended with the highlight, Founder's Ball. For that one evening, the hospital was run by as few staff as possible and everyone who could attend the Ball let their hair down and really enjoyed themselves. Even Matron had been known to unbend and smile benevolently on her young nurses as they danced and flirted with amorous doctors and medical students.

Kate had intended to devote this evening to study. She had neglected her books lately, but she cast them into the limbo of another day without a qualm. She was off duty the next day and so could spend the night at her Hampstead home. It would be nice to enjoy a quiet dinner with her father and listen to some of the music they both loved . . . and when her mother came in from the committee meeting they could have a long and intimate chat.

Kate looked forward to luxuriating in the comfort and privacy of her own room after weeks of sharing with Phyllida, who was a dear but frequently came in very late, via the ground-floor window that had apparently been used by nurses without late passes since time immemorial Home Sister Vernon was a lovable old duck, but she kept a careful eye on the comings and goings of her charges. It seemed strange that she did not know about the faulty catch on that window!

It was a very warm day. Kate was glad to relax in the sun for a few minutes after lunch before going back to work. The statue of Sir Henry presided over the small but pleasant square that was surrounded by tall hospital buildings. Its neat lawns and well-stocked flower beds provided a pleasing prospect for those patients whose wards overlooked the garden and it was a popular meeting-place for staff. The paved paths were used as short cuts from one building to another by nurses and doctors and a variety of hospital staff as well as patients and visitors.

The Preliminary Training School bordered the garden and on fine days such as this it was a common sight to see a group of girls with their books, animated and pretty in their crisp cotton frocks, enjoying a brief break from lectures. It was not so very long since Kate had been one of the Pets, as they were known, a very green girl for all her medical background. She had been nervous and excited about going on the wards and quite convinced that she would fail the preliminary examinations. She had not exactly sailed through them with the ease of some of her set, but at least she had survived, unlike one or two girls who had vanished without trace.

She enjoyed Accident and Emergency. There was so much going on, so much drama and excitement, comedy as well as tragedy. It was hard work, keeping the nurses constantly on their toes, and Sister Carmichael was an old-fashioned disciplinarian who kept the patients as well as her nurses strictly in order. She knew just how to cope with abusive drunks, or aggressive teenagers with outlandish clothes and weirdly-coloured hair, or indignant mothers who resented waiting for attention with crying children. She was warmly sympathetic and understanding with shocked old ladies and frightened children and bewildered motorists who automatically blamed the other driver for an accident. In the midst of it all, she organised the department with brisk and practical efficiency.

Kate felt that she was learning more about actual nursing on A and E than some of her friends on the wards, whose days seemed to revolve about bedmaking and bedpans. She might have been thrown in the deep end, but it was a challenge that she felt she could meet.

She glanced at the tiny gold watch that she wore pinned to the breast of her uniform frock. She was wearing her cap, but the white apron was a symbol of being on duty and she had taken it off before leaving the department to take her meal break.

Five more minutes. It was nice to relax, to ease her slightly aching feet, to enjoy a little of the sun before she went back to a predictably busy afternoon.

She did not look twice at the tall man in the white coat who walked briskly along the paved path towards the circular wooden seat about the base of the statue. White coats were much too familiar a sight to a hospital nurse to attract attention. After the flurry of the first few days, when every doctor seemed a very romantic figure, they merged with the scenery.

Todd paused beside her, smiled. He had not consciously looked for her as he crossed Main Hall and glanced through the open doors of A and E before pushing open the swing doors and emerging into the bright sunshine of the hospital garden. But he had felt a swift shaft of pleasure as he recognised the pale hair and trim figure of the girl who sat with hands lightly clasped in her lap and the hint of a smile just warming the lovely face.

'Very nice . . .' he drawled—and the words might have applied to the day, or the surroundings, or the girl.

Kate looked up, surprised and wary. There was a smile lurking in his eyes and she wondered if he was amused by her discomfiture. She felt hot as she thought of the way she had slapped him down without the least cause. She ought to apologise and explain, but she did not really want to mention her mistake. For it must have seemed an appalling conceit to suppose that Todd Morgan was interested in a girl he had never noticed until that morning.

'Beautiful,' she said stiffly, only just polite and not at all encouraging.

'Just what I was thinking,' he agreed, his smile deepening and admiration in his gaze. This time, there was no mistaking his meaning.

Kate was disconcerted, slightly embarrassed and very annoyed with the way the blood rushed into her face. She blushed much too easily and hated it! She rose to her feet. 'Time to get back to work,' she said briskly, sounding like Sister Carmichael.

'Running away?' His tone was gently teasing.

Her chin tilted at the implication that she could not handle the overtures of his kind. 'Sister will be looking for me,' she said firmly.

'I've been looking for you for most of my life,' he told her lightly.

Kate threw him a sceptical glance. 'If that's an opening gambit, then I don't think much of it!'

'It isn't as original as your approach, I must admit.' His blue eyes danced with mischief.

She bit her lip and turned away, refusing to admit that her heart was beating just a little faster at the look in those eyes, with its promise of delights that she had yet to know.

She thought that she thrust her father's note into her pocket as she hurried away. But, slightly flustered, her fingers quite missed the opening and the piece of paper fluttered to the path.

Todd moved to retrieve it.

'Just a minute, Nurse!'

He realised that he did not yet know her name. She ignored him, quickening her pace. Todd glanced carelessly at the sheet of paper, wondering if she had meant to throw it away.

He was used to skimming over medical notes and letters from GPs and gathering the gist without having to read every word. So he immediately recognised it as an invitation, from a man who cared about her, without really meaning to pry into her affairs.

'*Dearest Kate . . .*'

At least he now knew her first name. Sweet Kate, he thought, amused. Not so sweet Kate, in fact. Lovely face, superb figure—and a tart tongue. A shrew, it seemed—and he was not much inclined to play Petruchio to her Kate. There were more than enough women in the world. He did not need to waste time and energy in pursuing one who did not want him and showed it!

But she really was much too lovely to dismiss so easily . . .

'All your young doctors . . .'

It seemed that she was a popular girl, much in demand. Well, it was not surprising. Any man would respond to that cool, shining beauty and that virginal air. Just as he had.

'Take pity on a lonely man . . .'

Todd wondered if she would—and if she had been thinking of the writer who had penned the note as she sat in the warm sun with that little smile playing about her lovely lips.

He felt a sudden dislike of her involvement with the man who had written to her so warmly. He was no handwriting expert, no analyst, but it seemed to Todd that those words had been written by someone who was much older than the blonde girl. Some girls did prefer older men, of course, father-figures. But the lovely Kate ought not to throw herself away on an old man!

It seemed she was trying to end the affair. *'It's too long since we've seen each other . . .'* Any man would miss someone so lovely when she walked out of his life. Todd did not even know her, but he had been immediately aware of her irresistible appeal, her enchanting loveliness.

Todd knew that he would look out for her and seize the opportunity to talk to her in the hope of persuading her to go out with him one evening. He put the note away in his pocket for the time being. It would give him an excellent excuse for seeking her out. But it would have to wait until later. He was on his way to a conference with Sir Lionel and the other members of the team and he was already late . . .

Kate pinned on a clean apron and went to report to Sister Carmichael, determined not to think again about Todd Morgan. He was too smooth, too sure of himself, and she did not mean to be flattered by the fleeting interest of a man who was said to have just one thing in mind where girls were concerned.

That disturbing glow in his eyes was not a compliment, she told herself firmly. He looked at too many girls in just that way. It would be madness to believe anything he said. *Looking for her all his life!* Such nonsense! It was that warmly persuasive and much too ready tongue that had talked too many girls into bed, she suspected.

Kate was a virgin and she planned to stay that way until she found the one man she could love enough to marry. Perhaps it was an old-fashioned attitude, but she kept every man at a safe distance. She did not mind a few kisses, the warmth of an embrace, at the end of an enjoyable evening with a man she liked. But so far she had never liked any man enough to allow matters to go any further.

She was only nineteen. There was plenty of time to experience the doubtful delights of sex, she felt. Kate had yet to discover that there was anything particularly delightful in the hot and hungry kisses or the clumsily pawing hands of over-sexed young men who occasionally thought that she could be tumbled into bed as easily as some girls. She felt that she would need to be very much in love before her body responded to a man's kiss, a man's touch, a man's urgency of wanting. Until that day dawned, her body would remain her own.

Yet there had been that odd little quiver of excitement tingling down her spine when Todd Morgan put his hand briefly on her arm to steady her that morning. Her pulses had certainly quickened when he paused to speak to her in the hospital garden. And that strange, disturbing sensation she had known when he looked down at her with that warm smile and something more in his blue eyes might well have been the first stirrings of attraction.

Which made it all the more dangerous to go on thinking about Todd Morgan and wondering if he felt a genuine interest in knowing her, Kate told herself firmly—and tried to concentrate on a patient's account of the accident which had caused severe lacerations of his forearm. It was not easy to follow the broad Scots dialect of the young man who was working on a nearby building site. But she had no problem in understanding his admiration and invitation as she carefully swabbed blood and dirt from the cuts ready for examination and probable suture by one of the casualty officers.

Despite the accent, it was obvious that the Scotsman was paying her a great many heavy-handed compliments. Kate ought to be used to it, but she could still blush and sometimes she longed to sink through the floor with embarrassment. Some patients seemed to believe that they could say what they liked to a nurse, she thought wryly. Fortunately, most of them had a great deal of respect for the young girls who wore the uniform of a Hartlake nurse. Even so, the young and the pretty were at risk in a department like A and E that dealt with a wide cross-section of the population by day and by night.

His arm sutured and dressed, the Scot waylaid Kate before he left, telling her that she was a bonny wee lass and he would buy her a drink if she met him in the pub that evening.

She thanked him and refused politely, explaining that she was not allowed to date the patients. He insisted. Kate shook her head, smiling. Harmless but hot-headed, he put his good arm about her slender waist and tried to kiss her. The shock of his whisky-laden breath told her that he had been drinking from the bottle that bulged his jacket pocket.

Other patients watched in a kind of lethargy. Sister and the rest of the staff were apparently too busy to notice the incident.

'Please behave yourself, Mr McEwan,' Kate said firmly, trying to elude that strong, snaking arm and the grinning red face.

'Aw, come on, wee lassie . . . gie us a kiss afore I gannen ma way . . .'

Todd Morgan put a firm hand on the young man's shoulder. 'On your bike, Mac,' he said lightly, but with inflexible authority. 'The wee lassie has her work to do!'

The Scotsman angrily shrugged off the hand, glowering. He looked as if he might argue, but then changed his mind. Swaggering to show that he left of his own free will, he made his way across the tiled floor to the swing doors and out.

'Thank you,' Kate said stiffly, but grateful. Drunks were always an unknown quantity, after all.

'Any time . . .'

'I could have handled him, of course,' she told him. 'One gets used to dealing with that kind of thing in this department.'

'Of course,' he agreed, blue eyes twinkling. 'You were handling him very well. I noticed.' The teasing brought a blush to her lovely face. As she turned to move away, he put a restraining hand on her arm. 'Just a minute, wee lassie. I've something for you,' he said lightly, bringing the folded sheet of notepaper from his pocket and offering it to her with a flourish.

One piece of paper looks much like another. Kate did not even glance at it, let alone recognise it as her father's note that she firmly believed to be tucked into her pocket. She was suddenly indignant that it should amuse him to make her look foolish, to embarrass her.

'I haven't the time or the patience for silly games,' she said, ice tinkling in her tone. She snatched the note from him and tore it across.

Todd folded his arms across his broad chest and looked down at her, amused. 'You shouldn't jump to conclusions,' he drawled. 'I didn't write it. You dropped it in the garden and I'm merely returning your property.'

'Oh . . .!' Kate looked down at the shreds of paper and saw remnants of her father's handwriting. She glared at him. 'Couldn't you have said so?' she demanded crossly, feeling even more foolish.

'I wonder why you should suppose that I'm in the habit of writing notes to pretty girls,' he mused, eyes dancing. 'I do have a tongue in my head and when I meet a girl I like I don't hesitate to ask her to go out with me. Being a cautious man, I try not to put anything in writing,' he added humorously.

'I can believe that!'

He raised an eyebrow. 'That implies that you know much more about me than I know about you, Kate. I'm intrigued.'

'You're the one with the reputation,' she said, wishing her heart did not shake so foolishly at the sound of her name on his lips, at the warmth in his blue eyes. He was a very practised charmer and it would be madness to let him charm her into anything.

He nodded, laughter lurking. 'That's true . . . and forewarned is forearmed. At least you know that I'm not to be trusted. I shall make mad passionate love to you at the first opportunity that comes my way, of course. Something for us both to look forward to, Kate,' he said outrageously.

She would not smile, but amusement crinkled his eyes with disarming attractiveness and she could not help liking him or warming to him.

'Well, will you?' Todd asked swiftly as Sister Carmichael came out of a cubicle and looked about her for a nurse with idle hands.

'Will I what?' Kate was puzzled.

'Come out with me? Tomorrow night. A show and some supper and we'll dance the night away.' He smiled persuasively.

'I don't know,' she said slowly, tempted—and wondering why she was so tempted by a man that she did not know and ought not to trust.

Sister Carmichael glanced at the couple, a slight frown in her eyes. She suspected that they were indulging in non-professional conversation. It was quite impossible to keep the young from flirting at every opportunity, but she was surprised that someone as seemingly sensible as Nurse Murray should be encouraging a rake like Todd Morgan.

'Nurse!' she said, rather sharply.

'Yes, Sister. Coming, Sister!'

Never doubting instant obedience from a Hartlake junior, she did not wait to see if the girl ran at her bidding, but vanished into the cubicle once more with a flurry of curtains.

Kate would have been right on her heels if Todd Morgan's hand had not clamped firmly about her wrist.

He smiled into her eyes, very warm. 'Say yes, Kate,' he urged. His strong fingers did not hurt. But they did make her tingle from head to toe in the strangest fashion.

Prompted by a natural instinct for self-preservation, Kate had every intention of giving him a firm *no* and sticking to it. So she really did not know how it happened that she said, breathlessly: 'Yes—all right. Tomorrow night!'

'I suppose you live in? Being first-year? I'll meet you outside the Nurses' Home at seven-thirty if that suits.'

Then he was gone and it was too late to declare that she had changed her mind and really did not wish to spend any of her precious off-duty hours with a man whose amorous affairs kept the grapevine humming.

Kate hurried to join Sister Carmichael who needed assistance in the undressing of a very stout woman who had been sent from her GP for an electrocardiograph. It was suspected that she had suffered a slight heart attack as she busied herself with setting up her stall in the local street market earlier that morning. The poor woman was

sweating profusely and was in such a state of nerves that
she could scarcely speak or help herself at all. It was
obvious that she would need to be sedated before the
ECG could give a true reading of the state of her heart.
She would probably be admitted for rest and careful
observation.

Kate did not see Todd Morgan again that day. But he
was much on her mind and she was troubled by a
readiness to like him, to be drawn by the very physical
magnetism of the man. It would be naive to suppose that
he would wine and dine her and be content to end the
evening with a few chaste kisses!

Kate wondered if she should stand him up. She did not
have to hurry back to Hartlake to meet him, after all. A
snub of that nature must persuade any man of her lack of
interest. But she had always disliked that kind of thing.
It was cowardly not to turn up for a date instead of
turning down an invitation in the first place. She could
have said no to Todd Morgan very easily. She should
have said no, in fact. But as she had obeyed an absurd
impulse to agree to a date then she must do the decent
thing and meet him. At the same time, she must be very
careful to keep her head.

She did not see Todd as she got into her father's car that
evening. But he saw her. On his way to the Kingfisher,
regular haunt of many of the staff at Hartlake, he saw the
gleaming Rolls Royce and recognised the driver. He
paused, curious to know why it was waiting outside the
Nurses' Home.

He felt a shaft of dismay when Kate came out and
hurried to the car, coolly lovely in a silk floral suit and

carrying a suitcase. She slid into the passenger seat as Sir Terence opened the door, and smiled at him with unmistakable warmth. Then she leaned to bestow a light kiss on the consultant's cheek.

Todd walked on, hands clenched in his pockets. So Sir Terence had written that note to her! Well, he was a man like any other—even if he was reputed to be happily married—and it was not surprising that the lovely Kate should have caught his eye. But it was not very wise to be so blatant about that relationship. No fool like an old fool, of course.

Todd was more surprised that such a girl as Kate should lend herself to some kind of affair with a much older man. She had not seemed to him to be that kind of girl . . .

CHAPTER THREE

KATE was filled with a very foolish excitement for most of the day. Or was it just apprehension?

She changed her mind a dozen times about what to wear for her date with Todd Morgan. She went to the hairdresser so that her pale hair should look its very best—and promptly combed out the fashionable waves and curls when she arrived home. It had seemed too stiff, too obviously set for the occasion. She did not want him to think that she had taken any special pains for something that was just another date, after all.

Then she was very nearly late, arriving by taxi at the Nurses' Home only moments before his bronze-coloured Cortina drew up. She had been so pale that afternoon that her mother had demanded to know if she felt ill. Now, walking across the seemingly interminable stretch of pavement to the car, she felt that her face was aflame.

Todd leaned across to open the car door for her. All day, he had been in two minds about keeping the date. He had toyed with the irony of leaving a note for her at the Nurses' Home. A doctor could always find a satisfactory excuse for breaking a date and a nurse was not likely to question the sudden need to stand in for a colleague.

He had told himself that it was none of his concern if she was having an affair with Sir Terence. He had no right to disapprove or dislike her behaviour or her morals. Heaven knew that his own way of life could not stand up to close scrutiny and he refused to subscribe to old-fashioned double standards.

In truth, it was Kate's youth that bothered him. Sir Terence must be at least thirty years older than the girl. How could she go to meet him so happily, complete with overnight case in a way that told its own story? How could a girl with that deceptively virginal air, that charming look of innocence, lie in the arms of a man old enough to be her father? Todd was unexpectedly shocked and oddly disappointed in the girl who had stirred him at first sight.

She had been off duty all day. He had looked out for her, making an excuse to visit A and E, wondering at the appeal that drew him despite the discovery that she was not the delightful innocent she seemed. He had made it his business to learn that she was enjoying the day off and he was told that she had gone home for the night. Well, it was possible. But Todd thought it unlikely, recalling the way she had smiled at Sir Terence and leaned to kiss him.

'Kate . . .' he said, greeting her with a hint of stiffness.

She looked at him doubtfully. There was *something*, his failure to smile perhaps, or the rather stern expression in those very blue eyes. 'What's wrong?' she asked quickly.

Todd was surprised by her sensitivity. What did they know of each other, after all, that she could apparently gauge his mood in a moment?

'Not a thing,' he said lightly.

Kate did not believe him. But she was in the car and it seemed too late to scramble out, to call an abrupt halt to the evening before it properly began. But it seemed to her that he regretted the arrangement and her heart sank slightly.

'You look charming,' he said with a genuine admiration. She looked virginal, he thought, dryly. The white silk dress with its loose jacket over bare shoulders was very fashionable and probably more expensive than the average junior nurse could afford. A gift from her wealthy lover?

The clinging silk emphasised the shapely curves of her slim body, stirring his senses. The small face was delicate and appealing, flower-like in its cool loveliness. She looked beautiful and serene and he did not like to think of her in the arms of a fifty-year-old consultant.

'Thank you.' Kate, very conscious of him, felt stupidly shy. He was attractive, but almost aloof in the formal suit, dark hair burnished and sleek to the handsome head, capable hands on the driving wheel. She wished he would turn to look at her, smile. She might then feel more at ease with this tall dark stranger who did not seem to belong in her life. She wondered why she had spent almost all day in a state of nervous excitement because she was meeting a man who made her feel now that he regretted an impulsive invitation. 'Where are we going?' she asked brightly.

'I hope you like musicals. I managed to get seats for the new show at the Palace. We'll just have time for a drink first if parking isn't too much of a problem. Supper at Zimba's after the show, I thought. I've reserved a table.'

'You've gone to a lot of trouble.'

He had. He had wanted to impress her, to show that

he could give her a good time, to make her feel that an evening might be better spent with a young doctor with his name to make than with an elderly if successful specialist!

'Perhaps I shall be suitably rewarded,' he said lightly.

Kate stiffened. 'And perhaps you won't,' she said, equally light but with coolly unmistakable warning that he must not think of her as an easy conquest.

Todd shrugged, smiled. Women liked to play games, he knew. Most of them could be tumbled into bed at a touch, he had found. All of them liked to play hard to get or to pretend that they did not usually indulge in sexual encounters. In his experience, virgins were extremely rare birds.

He laid his hand over her clasped fingers, taut in her lap. 'Relax, Kate. Just enjoy the evening. It will end exactly the way you want it to, I promise.'

As a reassurance, it was double-edged, she thought. His touch was warm, disturbing. So was the look in his eyes. There was a confidence in his manner that she had not noticed before—and that was even more disturbing.

Was he so sure of getting what he wanted because she had impulsively agreed to go out with him? Had it been such a mistake to be swayed by the charm of his smile, the lure of his magnetism?

Kate knew that she liked him, perhaps too much. She felt sick with dismay and a lurching disappointment at the thought that it might be necessary to break off their friendship before it had even begun.

But it had been foolish to suppose that he might regard her as different from all the other girls he had known. She had not been given the least reason to think so, after all. And it was ridiculously naive not to know that if a man like Todd Morgan took a girl for an expensive night out, he expected her to end up in bed with him at the end of it. Knowing his reputation, she should have avoided him like the plague. Instead, she had encouraged him to believe that the evening would end just as he wished and just as he had probably planned!

She sat very still, very stiff, silent.

Todd, intent on manoeuvring the car in the steady stream of London traffic and keeping an eye out for a likely parking place at the same time, felt uncomfortably aware of her silence and her suspicion. It was not going to be a very successful evening, he thought wryly. She did not trust him and did not seem too sure that she liked him, either. And he was disappointed in her and finding it rather hard not to let it show.

They had to walk for some way through the narrow streets of London's theatreland from the only available parking place to the Palace Theatre. Kate's high heels slowed her down. Once, her heel turned on the uneven pavements. Todd reached for her hand and drew it through his arm. She knew it would be much too pointed to pull away, a disastrous start to an evening that seemed to hold so little promise, anyway.

'Sorry about this,' he said, looking down at her. 'Parking in town is absolute hell these days. A taxi would have been much more practical.'

'It doesn't matter,' she assured him coolly. 'Nurses are used to walking.'

'Not in shoes like those,' he said, very dry.

The words and the tone seemed scathing, and they

echoed in her head when they finally reached the theatre, making her feel that it was entirely the fault of her ridiculous shoes that there was no time for the drink he had planned, after all.

'We'll have one in the bar during the interval,' Todd promised as he escorted her up the wide, plushly-carpeted stairs to the circle.

Kate nodded, indifferent. There was a hard little lump of disappointment in her breast and she doubted if anything could redeem the evening. They were strangers with nothing in common and it seemed likely that they would remain so.

There was a mix-up over their seats. They were ushered into the wrong row and Todd, usually the most good-natured of men, was in the mood to be belligerent when he was challenged by two men who arrived just as the curtain was going up.

By the time the matter had been sorted out and they had been shown to the correct seats, Kate was ready to sink through the floor with embarrassment, feeling that all eyes were on them rather than the stage. It did not help that they and almost everyone else in the near vicinity had missed most of the opening number in the confusion.

Todd was furious. The evening seemed doomed to disaster. He stared at the stage, the whirling dancers in their colourful costumes and the stars of the spectacular show who were such favourites with the public. It was a smash-hit musical that he had particularly wanted to see, but he saw and heard very little of its first half as he sat beside Kate, disinclined even to reach for her hand.

Kate did not enjoy it very much, either. She was too

conscious of the man by her side and the occasional sidelong glance at the stern profile did not improve matters. It was obvious that he was annoyed, almost unaware of her or the happenings on stage. He had been made to look foolish and no one liked that, she thought with a stirring of sympathy.

She wished she knew him better and liked him more. Then it might have been easy to slip her hand into his arm, to smile and assure him that nothing could really spoil the evening, to draw him into some appreciation of the music and the action with a real concern for his enjoyment.

But he seemed to be very much a stranger and Kate could not help wondering what she was doing in his company. They seemed to have nothing going for each other, she thought ruefully, marvelling that she had thought him so attractive, so exciting.

The circle bar was crowded in the interval and it took some time for Todd to get the drinks and make his way back to Kate through the seething press of people.

She sipped the Martini, deciding not to depress him with the news that she had dropped the expensive programme he had bought for her and that her drink had not been diluted with lemonade as she liked. It was really much too strong for her taste—or her head, she thought warily.

'What do you think of the show?' Todd asked, polite. 'You seem to be enjoying it. Very good, don't you think? Lively . . .'

Kate looked up at him. He was so tall that even in her fated high heels she only just reached his shoulder with her blonde head. 'I don't think you've seen or heard any of it,' she said quietly, suddenly impatient with pretence.

'Of course I have,' he said lightly, on the defensive. He finished his whisky and wondered if there was time and if it was worth the effort to get himself another. He needed something to raise his spirits. People were still milling about the bar. Watching them, indifferently observing them, he suddenly remembered something. 'I had a box of chocolates for you!' he exclaimed. 'Part of the theatre tradition, isn't it? I left the damn things in the car!'

His expression was so rueful that Kate began to laugh. For it was so obviously the last straw! 'Oh, Todd! This just isn't your evening!' she declared, warmly sympathetic.

'You're right,' he agreed. Suddenly, he smiled at her, all the disappointment and dismay melting before the warmth in her lovely face and the sympathetic, understanding humour in those expressive eyes. And she had called him Todd! He had been doubting that she even knew his name! He put an arm about her shoulders and drew her against him in sudden liking. 'I'm sorry, Kate. I wanted it to be so right for you,' he said, meaning it.

Suddenly, it *was* right.

Kate smiled back at him, the sweet smile with just the hint of shy modesty that most men found so captivating. Todd was no exception.

When they returned to their seats and the lights dimmed for the second half of the show, he reached for her hand and Kate allowed it to lie in his clasp. Occasionally, he ran his thumb over the silky inner flesh of her wrist in a kind of caress that set her tingling. She was even more conscious of him than before, for now he turned frequently to smile, brushed her hair or her cheek with his lips in seemingly accidental encounter when he murmured some comment in her ear, pressed her hand warmly at moments of mutual appreciation of a certain song or an exciting dance routine.

There was a kind of intoxication in sharing the mood of an audience who responded so rapturously to the very successful musical. There was a kind of intoxication in the nearness of a very attractive man who let her know that she was very attractive to him, too.

Emerging into the night when the curtain finally fell, Kate was starry-eyed, a little dazed and a little drunk on the stirring and spell-binding music, the riot of colour and movement.

They ran for a taxi and tumbled into it, laughing, and Todd directed the cabby to take them to Zimba's, one of the newest and most exclusive nightclubs in town.

Then, with his arm about her, he turned Kate's face towards his own with his free hand and kissed her, so lightly that it did not seem right that her senses should tumble so wildly.

She drew back, eyes wide, heart thudding and that tingling excitement in all her veins, a little alarmed by her readiness to respond to the man she scarcely knew and had not yet made up her mind to like.

She looked so startled, so virginal, that Todd was shaken. How could any girl manage to look quite so innocent, so suddenly awakened by the merest of kisses, when all the evidence about her pointed to the contrary?

Deliberately, he thrust the thought of her and Sir Terence to the furthest recesses of his mind. He was damned if he would let that absurd dislike and jealousy of their relationship spoil the rest of the evening! It was all to the good if she was not a virgin, after all . . .

He bent his head to kiss her again, desire urgent in him. She put her fingers against his lips, swiftly.

'No . . .!' Kate did not trust the stirring of her senses. He was too attractive, too dangerous! She had a great deal to lose if she allowed this man to sweep her off her feet!

He kissed her fingers, a smile in his eyes, suddenly very sure that she was filling with a desire to match his own.

'I want you, Kate,' he said, direct. He saw her mouth quiver, saw the almost imperceptible shake of her head. He drew her close and brushed the smooth wing of pale hair from her lovely face. Ignoring the instinctive pressure of her hands against his hard chest, he tilted her face and laid his mouth on hers with a hint of smouldering passion. His long fingers trailed lightly down the slender throat to the gentle swell of her young, eager body in the thin frock. 'Lovely Kate,' he said, soft and sensuous against her lips, his hand closing gently over the soft curve of her breast.

Despite that melting warmth in the depths of her body and the delicious languour that stole over her at his touch, his kiss, Kate pushed him away firmly and sat straight and as far as she could get from him on the leather seat, trying not to tremble.

'Behave, Todd,' she said, firmly.

He smiled ruefully as the taxi came to a halt outside the brightly-lit entrance to the nightclub. 'The mood but not the moment,' he said softly.

Kate was too honest to deny the mood. But he need

not think that the moment to sweep her off her feet and into bed would come later that night, she told herself resolutely. She might be shaken and terribly tempted by his undeniable impact on her newly-awakened senses, but she was determined to keep a tight grip on her virginity.

Their table was in a secluded corner. The band played the kind of music that Kate had scarcely known that people still danced to these days . . . slow and dreamy and heart-stirring.

The food was delicious and the wine was heady and the music was as sensual as her mood as she danced in Todd's arms later that night.

He held her very close and their bodies only just moved to the music on the small and dimly-lit dance floor that lent itself to romance.

She could feel the heavy thud of his heart and wondered if he knew that it was in rhythm with her own. Their heads were very close, his cheek pressed against hers, and his body was tense, hinting at an urgency that ought to alarm her but did not. Kate supposed that all her earlier doubts and fears were allayed by the wine. She had probably drunk far more of it than was wise. She did not seem to care . . .

Euphoric, she liked the strength of his arms about her and she liked the touch of his warm lips on her hair, her eyes, her cheek. She liked the nearness of him and she liked what it was doing to her even if it was much too dangerous.

Kate was on the verge of a quivering and delicious excitement that could easily sweep her into an ecstasy that she had never known, but would surely discover in this man's ardent embrace. She melted against him in yielding, dreamy surrender, her arms about his neck, unconscious provocation and invitation in every line of her lovely body.

Todd drew her from the dance floor to their table. 'Time to take you home,' he said, a trifle unsteadily. She was almost too much temptation. It was strange that he was so much inclined to believe that her appeal was innocent, unconscious. She had that enchanting quality of innocence that must quicken any man's desire . . .

Like many of the medical staff at Hartlake, Todd had a flat in one of the tall terraced houses in Clifton Street, a narrow turning that ran alongside the hospital buildings.

A little light-headed and very sleepy, Kate drowsed in the car beside him and did not seem to notice that he turned into the side-street instead of taking her directly to the Nurses' Home. But as they mounted the stone steps to the front door, his arm about her waist, she did turn a slightly startled face to him.

'You need some black coffee,' he told her, reassuring.

'It's late, isn't it?' she demurred.

'Not so very late.' He turned the key in the lock, pushed open the door and ushered her into the narrow hallway.

'Where are we?' she demanded, suddenly suspicious.

'Just a few minutes from the hospital. Clifton Street,' he said reassuringly. 'I've a flat on the top floor.'

She looked at him doubtfully. 'Oh, yes . . .?'

'Trust me, Kate,' he said softly and brushed her hair with his lips.

'I don't . . .' But she followed him up the narrow

stairway. Inside his flat, she looked about her with interest and wondered how many girls had been lured to their fate in this very attractive bachelor pad. 'I think I had too much wine,' she said, sitting abruptly on the deep-cushioned sofa. 'My head's going round . . .'

'It's the altitude.' Todd grinned. 'All those stairs. Relax while I make some coffee . . .'

She shook her head, partly in refusal, partly to clear the swimming sensation. 'I don't think I want coffee, Todd. I think I feel sick . . .'

He went to her swiftly, concerned. 'Do you?'

Kate leaned back against the cushions and smiled up at him, suddenly bubbling with laughter. For this could not be the way he had planned it, she thought mischievously, tempted to tease him. 'Queasy,' she said, eyes dancing. 'Is there a doctor in the house?'

Todd laughed. Then he sat down beside her on the sofa, reaching for her wrist, his experienced fingers seeking for the pulse. 'It's a little fast,' he said, smiling.

It was faster for the touch of his hand and the warm smile in his blue eyes, Kate thought wryly. She was thankful that she was only slightly light-headed from the wine and the excitement of the evening. She still knew exactly what she was saying and doing, thank heavens!

'Not very romantic, is it?' she challenged, amused. 'You want to make love—and I feel sick!'

Meeting the lovely eyes with all the warm laughter in their depths, his heart stirred with an unexpected tenderness and liking. She was quite enchanting and he wanted her very much . . . and Todd thought that she was very near to surrender for all this light-hearted pretence of resistance.

'I can recommend a good old-fashioned cure for that,' he said softly and then he bent his head to kiss her, long and lingering.

Kate's heart began to race. So did the blood in her veins. She resisted the pressure of his mouth for a moment and then she kissed him back with a warmth that quickened him to swift and urgent desire.

CHAPTER FOUR

WITH gentle and experienced hands, he eased her body so that she lay full-length on the sofa and then he stretched himself beside her, kissing her little murmur of protest into silence. Kate's heart was hammering in mingled excitement and apprehension. She told herself that she could handle the situation, even as she reminded herself that she was unused to coping with men who had his degree of experience, his kind of reputation, his undeniable impact on a woman's emotions.

Her senses swam at his kiss. His hands were on her body, gentle and seeking, and shudders of delight rippled through her at his caress. His lean body was taut and urgent, heavy against her, betraying with the throb of desire that fierce need that found a swift echo in her own body.

Kate knew she was playing with fire. She ought to push him away before the magic in his kiss overcame all her resistance.

Todd sensed that resistance and wondered. Was he mistaken about this girl? Was she a virgin, after all? Her lips were warm and eager, leading him on. But her body seemed to shrink from the urgency in him as though she was a shy newcomer to the delights of sex.

He drew away and brushed the pale hair from her lovely face. 'I saw you last night, you know,' he said, striving for lightness. 'Getting into a Rolls Royce driven by Sir Terence . . .'

Kate was surprised by the unexpected mention of her father at such a moment. But she smiled at him, in blissful ignorance of his misconception of their relationship. 'Oh, did you? It was really rather convenient. He had to see a patient in Private Wing and so could pick me up. I went home with him and stayed the night. It was a welcome change from the Nunnery.'

Todd's eyes narrowed, darkened. She was quite brazen about the whole thing. He found it shocking. At the same time, it eased his mind. For it seemed that he need not hesitate to take her, after all. Kate was no virgin, no innocent to be coaxed over a very important threshold in her life. He ought to be relieved when his body was so urgent for her. He dismissed that fierce dislike of her association with another man that was akin to jealousy, tightened his arms about her and kissed her with a new intensity.

The tide of desire crashed over her in a fierce wave as his lips came down on her own. Her body seemed to respond to his expertise as though it was an expertly-tuned instrument of passion. She had never been nearer to drowning in the depths of a man's embrace than in those moments, and Kate held him close, senses whirling, body clamouring with that ache for the ecstasy and the fulfilment that he promised in the way he held her, kissing and caressing her towards the ultimate surrender.

But a last vestige of common-sense prevailed, for all the delicious response to his lovemaking, and suddenly she checked the hand that was at her breast, warm and urgent in caress. She twined her fingers in the thick dark curls of his hair and prevented him from kissing her again in that lingering and sensual and utterly exciting way.

She smiled into his searching eyes. As lightly as she could to break the spell that was binding them both too strongly, she said: 'I think I'd like that coffee, after all. Do you mind?'

Todd did mind. Very much. With her in his arms, his body craved the delight and the satisfaction of his senses. He was still, swamped with dismay and fighting a desire that was fiercer than he had ever known. 'Now. . . ?' It was a groan.

'Please . . .'

He released her and sat up, running his hands through his dark hair, struggling for control. It was amazing that a girl who seemed so virginal could be capable of such sensuality. As a lover, she was incredibly exciting. No wonder Sir Terence was prepared to take the risk of exposure and scandal for the delight of holding her in his arms!

Todd schooled himself to patience. There was plenty of time, he told himself. The rest of the night, perhaps. She was playing hard to get and he wondered if she knew that it increased his wanting almost beyond bearing, or if it was due to a misguided sense of loyalty to another man.

Kate, blissfully unaware of all that was in his mind, followed him out to the kitchen and watched as he reached for mugs and spooned coffee from a jar, waiting for the kettle to boil.

He smiled at her and Kate's heart seemed to turn over. He was so very attractive and so much nicer than she had ever supposed and she was still melting from those exciting moments in his arms.

'Sugar?' She nodded. He bent his dark head to kiss her lightly. 'You're sweet enough, surely,' he teased gently.

Kate laughed. 'Charmer!' Suddenly filling with a new and deeper emotion, she slipped her hand into his arm and leaned against him, looking up at him with warm eyes. 'It's been a lovely evening, Todd,' she sighed. 'I have enjoyed it . . .'

'It isn't over yet,' he said, softly, a promise in the words and in his blue eyes. He kissed her again, so sensually that she took sudden fright. Before, his kiss had been coaxing her into giving. Now, it seemed that it was insisting upon her surrender before the night was through.

Kate drew away, fighting the enchantment of that warm mouth on her own. 'It's almost over,' she said firmly. 'Have you looked at the time lately? I hope someone has left the usual window open or I shall be sitting on the doorstep all night. I daren't rouse Home Sister at this hour!'

Todd put his arms about her. 'I want you to stay with me, Kate,' he said quietly.

She trembled at the look in his eyes, the unmistakable longing in that deep voice. She moved out of his arms, shaking her head, too stirred by a desire that matched her own. She had to be sensible although she was terribly tempted. It was a big step for any girl to take for the first and only time in her life. Her virginity was a very precious thing.

'I can't do that,' she said, very firm. She did not dare to sound rueful. It would be construed as weakness, a hesitation to be overcome by his persuasions.

'Yes, you can. You were off duty all day. You went home and stayed the night. Simple!'

Kate looked down at her hands, finding it so very hard to disappoint him—and herself. 'It would be simple if I wanted to stay,' she agreed carefully. 'I don't . . .'

'Don't want me?' He was quick, gently mocking. 'I don't believe that, Kate.'

She would not look at him. 'I don't want to get involved.'

'You are involved,' he said, smiling. 'Do you think I don't know what your body wants when I hold you, kiss you?' He saw the colour flood into the delicately-sculptured face. He touched the hot cheek in a light caress. 'I want you, too, Kate.' His voice was soft, coaxing. 'Where's the harm?'

She was silent, much too shy to explain that her virginity was at stake and she did not want to lose it lightly to a man she scarcely knew, even if she did like him and find him disturbingly attractive.

It seemed a stubborn and unreasonable silence to Todd. He did not understand her reluctance in the wake of all that response. Sensing frustration and disappointment in store after so much promise, he said with sudden impatience: 'Must I say that I love you? Is that it? I'm damned if I know why women set such store on empty words before they'll climb into bed!'

Kate flinched from the shock of his words, the force of that unexpected and totally undeserved attack. She was hot with shame that he should cheapen her with such contempt—and she was furious that she had given him cause and opportunity to do so.

Feeling as though he had hit her, she turned and

walked into the sitting-room. Trying to control her trembling, the sudden and very real sickness in her stomach, she picked up her bag and thrust her feet into discarded shoes.

Todd intercepted her way across the room. 'Kate . . .'

She looked at him, eyes cold. 'Goodnight, Todd.' There was finality in her tone.

'Oh, come on now, darling,' he said warmly, impulsively, regretting words that had been born of frustration and a deep-rooted jealousy of any man who had known the warmth and sweetness of her before himself. He attempted to put an arm about her.

Kate slapped his face. That endearment, following on the hurtful words, seemed to insult her integrity and intelligence. His touch kindled her to fresh anger. 'Don't treat me like some cheap tart!' she flared furiously, welling with hurt and humiliation.

The marks of her fingers stood out whitely against his bronzed cheek. His eyes were very dark and a nerve jumped in the lean jaw. 'Then you shouldn't behave like one,' he said quietly, taunting her with the inexplicable association with a much older man.

Kate caught her breath. Then she slapped him again, hating him. She wrenched at the door and ran from him, risking life and limb on the steep stairs in her high-heeled shoes.

The streets weren't empty even at that hour. There was some traffic and some late-night revellers. It was a somewhat seedy area and Kate did not really like walking by herself at night, even beneath the street lamps of the High Street. Recently, a nurse had been dragged into the shadows by a drunk and only her screams and a great deal of resistance had saved her from serious assault.

That night, Kate was too angry and too upset to notice or care that footsteps followed as she sped towards the Nurses' Home, thoroughly wretched and near to tears and chilled in her thin frock. She gasped in alarm as a hand caught at her arm, spun her round, her heart seeming to stop with fear.

'Kate, I'm sorry!' Todd's deep voice was urgent, contrite. 'I don't know what got into me. I don't usually treat women in that way.'

'Don't lump me with your other women!' she flared, shaking off his hand.

'Okay! I'm sorry!' he said again, wryly. 'I seem to be saying all the wrong things this evening!'

'Then don't say anything else. I don't want to hear it! Just leave me alone!' She walked on, angry and proud. Todd fell into step beside her. She ignored him. Reaching the main door of the Nurses' Home, she raised a hand to ring the night bell that would certainly wake Sister Vernon.

Todd checked the movement with a hand on her arm. 'Just a minute, Kate . . .'

She shook off his hand, angry. 'Will you go away!'

'I want to talk to you.'

'Well, I don't want to talk to you! I don't want to know you any more, Dr Morgan! I just wish tonight had never happened!' She was bitter, angry with the way she had responded to him and the way he had interpreted that response.

'But it did—and it wasn't all bad,' he said gently. 'Some of it was so good that I'll never forget it.' She looked at him swiftly, doubtfully. He smiled down at her. 'Don't walk out on me, Kate—please! I want you more than any girl I've ever known.' He cradled her face in both strong hands. 'You're special, Kate,' he told her softly.

The militant sparkle in her eyes began to fade. She wanted to believe him. She was afraid to trust him. She was not yet ready to forgive him. But she allowed him to brush her lips with his own, very briefly. Then she drew back, wary. 'I won't be your mistress,' she warned bluntly, heat in her face and glad of the shadows. 'If it's all you have in mind then let's finish here and now, Todd.'

'It isn't. I want us to be friends,' he said quietly.

She thought of the surging passion and the ardent sensuality of this man. 'That won't be enough for you.'

'No, it won't,' he agreed wryly. 'But it has to be your choice, Kate. I'm not going to pressure you.' He hesitated. 'I'm not asking to be the one and only in your life,' he went on carefully. 'I know there's another man, and I can't promise that there won't be other women for me. But let me see you sometimes. Let's begin with liking and see where it leads.'

'You're very persuasive . . .'

'But you aren't persuaded.' He sighed. It had not been easy for him to swallow his pride and admit that this girl above all others stirred him to more than fleeting physical desire. He wondered if he had said too much or too little and if any of it had been the right words.

'I don't know. Give me time to think about it . . .'

He nodded. 'Of course.' At least it was not outright rejection, he thought thankfully.

On impulse, Kate touched her hand to the cheek she had struck, regretful. He tensed and then turned his head to kiss her fingers. She took instant fright at the way her heart responded to him. 'I think it might be as well if we don't see each other again,' she said.

'You thought too quickly,' he reproached, smiling.

'You don't understand . . .' She broke off. How could she explain the fear that she would become too fond of him, only to lose him to the next girl who came along? She did not want that kind of heartache.

'Yes, I do. You aren't trusting me,' he said ruefully.

'Too many girls have trusted you.'

'A man must sow his wild oats,' he said lightly to hide the dismay that she seemed so determined to keep him out of her life when his every instinct declared that he belonged in it.

'And it's his own fault if he doesn't like the harvest,' Kate retorted, fighting the impulse of her foolish heart with the natural caution of her level head. 'You know what everyone says of the girls who go out with you—justified or not! I don't want to be tarred with the same brush!'

'You've made your point!' he said, quick and angry. 'Goodnight, Kate.' He turned and walked away.

Kate looked after him, dismayed. She had done the right thing, the only sensible thing. But there was cold comfort in common-sense when the only man she might ever want seemed to be walking out of her life . . .

She was suddenly very weary, very cold and thoroughly dispirited. Again she turned to rouse Sister Vernon, longing to get to bed and forget the whole evening in sleep.

Before she could ring the bell, the door was opened and Patti Parkin, one of her flatmates, drew her in, smiling. Kate stared at her friend in surprise.

'I thought you'd never be done talking on the doorstep!' Patti exclaimed. 'I came in late, too. I was just closing the bathroom window when I saw you coming along the street with Todd Morgan in hot pursuit. I've been waiting all this time to let you in!'

'Thanks. I'm grateful.' Kate turned to the stairs.

'Is there something going on between you two that I ought to know about?' Patti demanded lightly. 'I didn't know that you were even friendly with our dashing Dr Morgan!'

Kate smiled briefly. It was late and she was tired and not at all inclined to go into details about an evening which, like the curate's egg, had only been good in parts. 'I hardly know him,' she said carelessly.

Patti was a dear, warm-hearted and kind, and she knew more about heartache than most people. But Kate did not want to talk, even to Patti, about that sick dismay in the region of her heart which was like nothing she had ever known before. She did not even want to think about it . . .

Hard work was a certain cure for it, she told herself, glad that they were so busy in A and E. There was very little time to hope for a glimpse of Todd, a few words with him, or a brief exchange of smiles. She might not see him for days and by then she would surely have conquered that foolish hankering for a Casanova who had proved that he really did have only one thing in mind where any girl was concerned, she told herself firmly, refusing to remember the warm and eager request for her friendship that she had chosen to spurn.

He had nearly seduced her, she reminded herself—and the alarming thing was that he had swept her to the point of surrender without really trying! Kate had tried to blame the wine. But she was too honest. She knew that her own weakness for the man was to blame, Todd had only to smile, to reach for her hand, to touch his lips to her own and she would be lost all over again. Something in her blood and in her body stirred too easily in response to him. Like too many girls, she had fallen for that charm, that charisma. She knew that she must keep him safely at a distance if she valued the virginity that she had always determined to cherish until her wedding day.

It seemed that there was going to be no need to fight him off, however. With every opportunity in the world to do so, he did not try to see her or speak to her. As the days passed, Kate found that she missed him and she began to feel that she would even welcome a note from him!

She had rebuffed him too successfully. Or the notoriously fickle Dr Morgan had turned his smiling charm on another girl. Heaven knew there were plenty to choose from at Hartlake and Kate was too modest to suppose that she had really counted as something special in his life. One evening, with its good and bad patches, did not make for a lifetime of loving—on either side—she told herself very firmly.

But her heart was inclined to rebel. And it insisted on fluttering like a captive bird in her breast when she saw Todd in Main Hall, some days after that evening. He had his back to her, but there was no mistaking that dark head, that set of broad shoulders in the white coat, that heart-wrenching curve of a bronzed cheek that she had slapped in anger.

Kate came to a sudden, startled halt, almost whisking the intravenous drip from the arm of a patient who was being wheeled on a trolley to Theatres, having lost a great deal of blood in a traffic accident. She was carefully carrying the plastic bottle of plasma and his folder.

'Watch out, Nurse!'

The sharp voice of the porter brought her to her senses. She murmured a hasty apology, bent over the patient to hide her flushed face and quickened her step to keep up with the trolley as it was trundled across Main Hall to the waiting lift.

'What's up with little Nurse Murray?' Jimmy said curiously. 'She don't seem to be herself at all lately.'

Todd turned swiftly. 'Who?'

'Nurse Murray. The little blonde on A and E. Pointed her out to you the other day, didn't I?' Jimmy's eyes twinkled. He had not missed the young houseman's sharpened interest in the pretty nurse.

'Murray?' Todd realised that he had never known her name until that moment. He swiftly wondered if he had misunderstood her attachment to the specialist with the same name. 'Any relation to Sir Terence?'

Jimmy grinned, laid a finger along the side of his nose in the age-old gesture of mystery. 'Do you see a resemblance?' he asked cannily. He was not one to break a promise. If people jumped to the right conclusion, well and good. But no one could claim that he had not kept his word. If it was getting to be common knowledge that she was Sir Terence's daughter then it was not his fault.

It was sufficient answer, Todd felt. The lovely Kate was as fair as Sir Terence was dark. He knew that Jimmy would have said soon enough if there was any relationship between them. No reason why he should not! The name could only be coincidence and it might explain why the consultant had first taken an interest in a girl who was so much younger than himself, but so lovely, so appealing, that any man must want to know more of her.

Just as he had, Todd thought wryly. He wished it had worked out. It was strange that he should think about her so much, miss her so much, when she had played such a small and brief part in his life. She seemed to be haunting him, day and night. It was much too soon to wonder if he had fallen in love at last. But it did seem that he might never cease to want her with a fierce, insistent desire that was a fever in his blood. He wondered, a trifle wryly, if Sir Terence or some other man was the reason why she would not allow herself to want him.

Jimmy turned away to answer a query from a patient. Todd moved away from the desk, on his way to the ward, and found himself in the path of a staff nurse. Tall and slim, dark of hair and eye, Elinor Nicholls was a friend.

She paused, smiled. 'Hallo, Todd.'

'Hallo, Nell.' He was pleased to see her. They had enjoyed an on-off relationship for some time, never very serious, never quite unimportant to either. They were more than friends and far from lasting lovers. 'How are you? Where are you working? I never seem to see anything of you these days.'

'Paterson.' She added, lightly: 'You know my name,

address and telephone number. I'm easily found.'

'And busy with a new love,' he reminded her, smiling.

'Not any more. Paul and I split up.'

'I didn't know.'

She shrugged. 'Then the grapevine isn't as efficient as usual.'

'I'm sorry.' He wondered if she had been hurt.

'I'm not. He was getting to be a drag. Took things too seriously. Not like you, Todd . . .' There was warmth, a hint of coquetry, in the fine dark eyes.

'We must get together again,' he said, almost meaning it. For perhaps he could erase the need for Kate in Elinor's familiar and welcoming embrace.

'I'd like that,' she said with truth. She hesitated and then laid a hand on his arm. With a man like Todd, one had to strike while the iron was hot, pin him down! 'Jo Laidlaw is giving a party tonight. I'm invited. Why don't you come with me? It should be fun . . .'

Todd didn't know why he hesitated. Surely he did not mean to turn celibate simply because one girl did not want him! 'Sure,' he decided, smiling. 'It sounds a great idea!'

Elinor smiled at him, quick and warm . . .

On her way back to A and E, Kate saw them together, the tall and very attractive doctor and the dark-haired staff nurse. She saw that he had said something to please the woman. It was written all over her as she smiled into his eyes.

It hurt to see the way that Todd responded with that smile, that glow in his eyes. It hurt to think of the staff nurse in his arms, knowing the kiss, the caress, the softly murmured persuasions that had delighted her so much—

and somehow she did not doubt that it would happen. It was written all over him!

Kate wondered why she liked a notorious rake who turned so nasty when he was thwarted. He was not looking her way. But her chin went up and she pinned a bright smile to her lips just in case Todd Morgan or anyone else supposed that she cared a damn about him!

CHAPTER FIVE

KATE sat at the book-strewn table, trying to work. But her mind refused to concentrate for long on the nervous system, the subject of that evening's study for Sister Tutor. It kept conjuring visions of Todd Morgan with a variety of girls, just to torment her.

It was absurd to be so bewitched by a man she hardly knew, but she could not stop thinking about him. She told herself that she had very little reason to like him—and knew that she had come disastrously near to falling in love with him!

It was just as well that she was not likely to have anything more to do with him. For one thing, he had lost interest in a girl who led him on only to disappoint him at the last moment. For another, it was no part of her plans for the future to become involved with a worthless Casanova who had a reputation for casual affairs that left a great deal of heartache behind them.

She was not dependent on a man like Todd Morgan for male admiration and attention, thank heavens! There were other men who liked her and sought her company, men who were entirely reliable and content with a virtually platonic relationship. Or, if not wholly content, at least they did not lose their tempers and insult her when she thwarted their attempts to lure her into bed!

It was true that Todd had rushed after her to apologise

and plead that they should be friends if nothing more. Kate could not help feeling that no man swallowed his pride to that extent unless a girl mattered to him. But that was dangerous thinking and obviously false. For if she was so important, why did he now ignore her and flirt so openly with other girls?

'*I know there's another man . . .*' he had said—and Kate had racked her brain to remember what she could have said or done to make him think that.

Of course, there were one or two special friends in her life, men such as Keith Anthony or William Palmer who had been regular escorts and companions since she had been at Hartlake. But they *were* only friends. Someone must have said something to Todd to convince him that further pursuit of her was pointless because she was in love with another man—and she could scarcely go to him and tell him that he was wrong and that she was free to love and be loved.

Anyway, she might be free, but she had no desire to love a man like Todd Morgan only to have him break her heart. He would take everything she was fool enough to give him and kiss her goodbye as soon as his fickle fancy was caught by someone else.

She sighed, so heavily that Phyllida looked up from the little dress she was smocking for her sister's baby girl.

'Something wrong?'

'I'll never make a nurse,' Kate said wearily. 'Ward-maid would have been a more suitable career, I'm beginning to think! I can cope with the practical work, just about, but these beastly books will defeat me, I know!'

It was easier to blame the pile of books with their

daunting contents for her depression than admit the folly of a heart that could not stop hankering after a worthless man.

At nineteen, it would be stupid to believe that she had met the only man she would ever love or want, she told herself firmly. At nineteen, she would probably fall in and out of love a dozen times before she met the one man she would really want to marry and be with for the rest of her life.

Todd Morgan was just a passing fancy. He was important only because she had discovered the excitement and the dangers of sex in his arms. He was the first man to stir her senses with his kiss and tempt her to throw all caution to the winds with his skilled and sensuous lovemaking. All the more reason to keep well out of his way, Kate told herself firmly—or she might wake up one morning to the dreadful discovery that she had parted with her precious virginity to a man who made a hobby of seducing innocents!

Instantly sympathetic, Phyllida put aside her needlework: 'We'll do it together,' she offered. 'It might help . . .' She was a quick learner with a retentive memory and she felt for those of her set who had problems with lectures and text-books and the long lists of bones and muscles and nerves which had to be learned. It was very necessary study, but it could be hard on a girl who had every attribute for nursing except the ability to cram her brain with a number of important facts in a very short time.

Her problem was very different. Phyllida was hopelessly accident-prone. If there was a thermometer to be dropped, a feeding-cup to be spilled, a trolley to be upset when it was laid-up in readiness for dressing or injection or suture removal, someone to be barged into as she emerged from kitchen or sluice or linen cupboard, then Phyllida was your girl! She was the despair of her seniors and a comedy turn to her fellow juniors on the ward.

Yet she promised to be a very good nurse in other ways. She was hard-working, conscientious, caring and she seemed to have an instant rapport with the sick and despairing. It was an impetuous and impulsive eagerness to please, to be of use, to prove her worth that was poor Phyllida's downfall. Wanting to do the work of a dozen nurses on the ward, she seldom had enough time to finish her own properly because she was constantly having to clear up after silly and irritating accidents. None so very serious that she was a danger to the patients, but any one of them enough to make a sister or staff nurse exclaim in exasperation that she would never make a nurse.

'I've a much better idea,' Patti declared, coming out of the bathroom with her auburn curls wrapped in a towel. 'Come to Jo's party with me and leave that lot for another night! All work and no play makes Kate a dull nurse!'

'Don't think I'm not tempted,' Kate said, wryly.

'Then come!' Patti rubbed at her wet hair, clinging in tight curls to her pretty head. 'Jo's parties are always fun and you know she'll welcome you. The more the merrier is her motto!'

At twenty-three, Patti was rather older than most of the girls in her set, having come late to nursing. Pretty and popular, her close friends at Hartlake, other than her flatmates, were second- and third-year nurses. But the friend who was throwing the party, Joanne Laidlaw, was training to be a physiotherapist. She had started at Hartlake as a student nurse only to discover that she turned faint at the sight of blood. Wanting very much to be involved in hospital work, she had turned promptly to physiotherapy.

Kate still hesitated. 'I ought to keep at these wretched books,' she demurred.

'You'll work better for a break. Study tomorrow,' Patti urged.

In truth, Kate needed little persuasion to bundle her books together and sweep them out of sight. A party might lift her spirits and take her mind off Todd Morgan—and there were always plenty of attractive men at Jo's parties! She might meet someone much nicer and more reliable than the rakish houseman. She hurried to get ready, wondering what to wear . . .

Patti extended the invitation to Phyllida but she was firm in refusing. 'I want to finish this frock before the baby grows out of it,' she said lightly.

Patti paused to admire the delicate and skilful smocking, marvelling that someone so noted for her clumsiness was capable of such exquisite work.

Kate settled for a long, flowered skirt, vivid colours on a black background, and a filmy black blouse with a scoop neckline and long, full sleeves. She looked very lovely with pale hair softly framing her face, and much more alluring than she knew.

When they arrived, the party was in full swing, drinks flowing and music almost drowning the hubbub of talk and laughter. Losing Patti almost immediately in the crowd, Kate was thankful to see some familiar faces. She was disappointed that Todd was not among them, although she knew he was one of Jo Laidlaw's many friends.

Several men made a bee-line for Kate. One of them was adept at getting rid of rivals and soon manoeuvred her into a reasonably quiet corner. 'I do know you, don't I?' he said, confidently.

Kate laughed. 'Kate Murray,' she obliged.

He grinned. He was as blond as herself and very good-looking. 'David Montgomery.'

'Yes, I know.' He was a registrar, a member of Professor Wilmot's team, and he was reputed to be a very good surgeon. She smiled at him with warm friendliness. 'I've seen you around.'

'Then you're a nurse? I thought so.' It had seemed more than likely. Most of the girls at the party were from Hartlake.

David found it more convenient if his girl friends knew and understood the demands that were made on a busy doctor in a big teaching hospital. Long hours and intense concentration on ward or in theatre or clinic meant that he needed to relax and unwind at the end of the day. He had discovered that girls who were not nurses did not understand or make allowances for the unexpected emergency that could disrupt his plans at the last moment. That kind of thing had ruined many a promising relationship. Now, he only pursued nurses—and there were plenty of opportunities for the kind of pursuit that he enjoyed at Hartlake.

He was working towards a consultancy and, like many ambitious young doctors, had no thought of marriage for the time being. But he knew that he would eventually marry one of the nurses in his life. For they would have common ground on which to build a lasting relationship and a mutual and very necessary understanding of the demands and difficulties of a doctor's life.

Briefly between girl-friends, he had been immediately attracted to the cool loveliness of this girl who seemed unattached—and taken immediate steps to remedy the matter.

'A fairly new nurse,' Kate said lightly. 'I've only been nursing for about three months.'

'Three months at Hartlake! And I haven't met you until now! Where have you been hiding that lovely face all this time?' His smile was warm, very admiring.

'On A and E—if you call that hiding. I don't! It seems a very public place to me!' Kate found her attention straying to some late arrivals at the party, her heart lifting with a foolish little hope that Todd might be one of them. He was not. She turned back to David Montgomery.

'. . . my work doesn't take me to A and E very often,' he was saying. 'But I shall make a point of visiting it frequently in future.'

Kate smiled at him. 'It's almost time for the change-over. I shall probably be transferred to one of the wards,' she warned.

'Make it one of my wards,' he said promptly. 'I want to see a lot of you, Kate Murray—on and off duty!'

He had a great deal of charm. Kate wondered why he was failing to charm her at all. He was very good-looking, very personable. There were plenty of girls at that party who would probably welcome his admiration, his attention, his obvious intent. Kate quite liked him. It wouldn't really matter to her if she never saw him again.

It did not seem that Todd was going to be at this party. Perhaps he was on duty. Perhaps he was enjoying himself elsewhere. Perhaps he would ignore her if he was present. Well, she had only herself to blame if he had decided to forget all about her, she told herself firmly.

It was almost impossible to dance in that crowded space. But people were dancing to disco music and Kate was drawn into their midst by a smiling David Montgomery. She had grace and a natural rhythm and she loved to dance. She discovered that he was an expert and something of an exhibitionist. To her dismay, they promptly became the centre of attention, other guests moving good-naturedly out of their way.

Kate was abruptly covered in shy confusion, hating to draw attention to herself. The soft blush that suffused her delicate skin from the roots of her hair to the tantalising curve of her breasts gave her an added loveliness. There was a great deal of admiring appreciation in David's eyes and some openly envious comment from his watching friends.

Flushed and breathless, Kate retreated, laughing and shaking her head to David's urging to dance on. It was at that moment that she saw Todd, standing by the door with a drink in his hand and a careless arm about the dark-haired staff nurse.

He was watching her intently—and it was impossible to read the expression in those very blue eyes. Meeting them, her heart lurched so violently that she thought he must know it. She looked away quickly, terrified of betraying that impact on her emotions, far from ready to admit how pleased she was to see him and how dismayed she was by the sight of his attractive and elegant companion.

Called to an emergency on one of the wards, Todd had been late in calling for Elinor at her flat—and she had seen to it that they were later still in leaving for the party. He had seen Kate as he walked into Jo's flat—and almost walked out again! For she was much too lovely . . . and she was dancing with David Montgomery in a way that implied that they had danced together many times.

With Elinor to consider, he had stayed, kissed Jo in warm and friendly greeting, acquired a drink and talked to various friends while Kate danced with the man whose admiring eyes were intent on that lovely face. Todd supposed that the registrar was yet another of the men in her life. He could not blame any man for wanting her, he thought wryly. He had been consumed with wanting since the first day that he had looked up in Main Hall and seen her, so young and pretty and shining with that apparent innocence.

Todd saw that she was suddenly embarrassed by the realisation that all eyes were on them as she danced with Montgomery. He watched the slow tide of colour in her lovely face and thought on a surge of tenderness that she must be the only girl he knew who could still blush—and she did it beautifully!

Kate backed from David, smiling, shaking her head. Turning, she looked directly into Todd's eyes. He meant to smile. She glanced away too soon and he thought that some of her enjoyment in the evening had fled at sight of him. Did she dislike him so much these days? Had he blown it so completely?

Elinor spoke to him and he brought his attention back

to her, smiling. A man knew where he was with a girl like Elinor. Warm, undemanding, good-natured and understanding, she knew a man's needs and how to satisfy them. Whereas Kate was a tease, full of promise and then letting a man down at the last moment. A girl who blew hot and cold in that fashion was no good for a man with his ardent, sensual nature. A man knew where he was with someone like Elinor . . .

Yet that half-hour in her arms had left him feeling oddly unsatisfied, even angry that the persistent need for one woman had driven him into the arms of another.

He ought to be able to put Kate out of his mind. She had only been a brief interlude with a disappointing outcome. Somehow, it was impossible. Todd could not and would not accept that those few kisses were all that he would ever know of her warmth and sweetness and delight.

Some minutes later, he made his way to the makeshift bar to get Elinor another drink. It was that kind of party. No one played host. Everyone had brought a bottle and it was a case of look after oneself or stay thirsty. Todd saw that David Montgomery was dancing with Jo and that Kate was standing by herself, watching, sipping a drink. Smiling, she looked relaxed and happy and very lovely.

Abruptly, Todd changed course.

Kate's hand tightened about the stem of her glass. Much too aware of him ever since she had realised his presence, she knew he was making for her—and pretended that she did not, her heart beginning to thud with a mingling of excitement and apprehension.

She wished he would keep away for all the wishing of

the past few days to see him, to talk to him, to know the touch of his hand. She did not trust him at all. She did not trust what he did to her uncertain emotions, turning them topsy-turvy with a glance, a smile.

Todd reached her side. She did not look at him. He saw that the smile that she kept pinned to her lips had faded from her eyes. He was dismayed.

'Don't ignore me, Kate. I'm not a stranger,' he said, direct.

She looked then, quick, slightly on the defensive. Did he expect her to fall on his neck with glad cries because he had chosen to notice her? He was here with another girl, wasn't he? Making a great deal of her, too! There was absolutely no reason why he should know that her heart was rushing around in a frenzy of delight because he had finally crossed the room to speak to her! Where was her pride, for heaven's sake! She needed someone like Todd Morgan like a hole in the head!

'You aren't exactly a friend, either,' she retorted coolly, still smarting from the fact that he had ignored her for days.

Todd decided to play it light, seeing the slightly stormy expression in her lovely eyes. 'As I recall, we passed that stage rather quickly,' he said, his eyes full of teasing reminder. She blushed slightly. Todd smiled with sudden, disarming warmth.

'Too quickly!' she countered.

He looked down at her, thoughtful. 'It could be. Something went wrong that night, certainly. We didn't get to be lovers.'

She quivered with a little outrage that he had thought it an inevitable outcome of their date. Didn't he know that she wasn't that kind of girl? 'Well, that wasn't the end of the world!' she said, chin tilting.

'It could have been the beginning of a wonderful new world,' he told her softly, meaningful warmth in his deep voice. 'I've missed you, Kate . . .'

Despite the fact that he took her name and turned it into an endearment, despite the way he looked and spoke and smiled, Kate did not believe him.

He was too smooth, too practised a charmer—and hadn't he arrived at this party with the dark-haired staff nurse clinging to his arm as if they were lovers? They probably were!

Her chin tilted slightly. 'You didn't miss me for long,' she said, and turned to David as he came back to her side at just the right moment. Her smile might not have been so warm, so welcoming, so very encouraging if she had not been set on convincing Todd that she hadn't missed *him* at all.

'I hope you aren't after my girl,' David said, punching his friend lightly on the shoulder.

'Todd, darling! What happened to my drink?' Elinor claimed him at the same moment, her manner warning off a girl she had been assessing from the other side of the room for some minutes.

She suspected that the blonde girl was attracted to Todd. But she did not consider her to be a threat. She was much too young for Todd's taste, Elinor decided confidently. He liked his women to be mature, experienced.

One only had to look at the undeniably pretty but very youthful girl to observe the shining, dreamy-eyed innocence that might initially attract but would soon begin to bore someone like Todd. And it was obvious that she wouldn't have a clue how to handle his sensuality . . .

Elinor swept Todd away to dance with a careless confidence that implied their intimacy—and Kate was grateful for the admiring attentiveness of another man to which she could respond as though she did not mind at all that Todd was so obviously involved with the staff nurse.

She danced a lot, mostly with David. She laughed and talked a lot with David and his friends. She seemed to enjoy herself a lot that evening.

In truth, she was longing for the party to come to an end. There was little pleasure in being with someone as nice, as attentive, as seemingly trustworthy as David Montgomery when she might have been with the sensual, unreliable, quick-tempered and notoriously fickle Todd Morgan who was paying far too much attention to someone else.

Kate did not want or expect him to neglect the woman for her sake, of course. She knew how she would feel if a man took her to a party and promptly deserted her for the attractions of another girl. She had no desire to be singled out by someone like Todd Morgan so that her name was bandied about all over Hartlake as his latest conquest, she told herself firmly.

But she could not help feeling that he might have given her more than those few minutes, too quickly interrupted. Not once had he caught her eye, smiled, asked her to dance with him or even shown that he resented her response to another man's attentions.

She hadn't been very encouraging to him, she admitted fairly. She had scarcely smiled and her attitude had been cold, snubbing. Why should Todd or anyone else suppose that she liked him too much for comfort when she wouldn't even show that she liked him at all!

David became involved in a light-hearted argument with a couple of medical students and Kate was free to look about her. Looking about her proved to be a mistake, for her glance instantly sought and found Todd, sitting in a chair with Elinor Nicholls on his knee, his arm about her waist and their heads much too close together. Whatever he was saying to the staff nurse, it made her smile with pleased delight and brush his lean cheek with her lips.

Kate looked away, filled with a fierce dislike of the woman and their obvious intimacy. She knew she was jealous. She was rather dismayed to discover how much it hurt that Todd was making light love to another woman.

How could she ever believe what was in his eyes, his smile, his touch? It was only too obvious what he wanted from any woman.

CHAPTER SIX

SHE pushed through people to the door, needing to escape, to be alone for just a few minutes. No one would notice if she left the party and she really did need some air. It was much too hot, too stuffy, too noisy and crowded. Perhaps Jo's party was a great success. Everyone else seemed to think so, anyway.

Kate wished she had not impulsively agreed to Patti's suggestion. She wished she had not seen Todd with the dark-haired staff nurse, his pursuit of the woman making an utter nonsense of the way he had smiled and looked when talking to her for those few minutes. She wished she had never known that he could be more than just an easily-dismissed and rather contemptible Casanova. She wished she did not like him so much . . .

Landing and stairs were almost as crowded as the first-floor flat. All the flats were rented to Hartlake nurses and most of them who were off duty that evening had drifted into the party, some to stay.

A window stood open at the end of the landing, leading out to a fire escape. Kate made her way to it and went out to the iron balcony between the flights of stairs, up and down. She was rather surprised that it was unoccupied, but there was a chill in the air. She was glad of the breeze that cooled her face and ruffled her soft hair as she leaned against the rail, looking at the star-studded sky and trying to blot out that hurtful image of Todd with his arm about Elinor Nicholls.

Someone put a hand on her shoulder. Without even turning, Kate knew it was Todd. Her body, her blood, recognised his touch. Her heart quickened and she tingled all over with that dangerous excitement. He had followed her! He did want to be with her if only for a snatched moment!

'I saw you slip out of the room and thought you looked rather pale. Are you all right?' he asked, warm with concern.

He brought his head low to look into her face and his breath was warm and sweet against her cheek. Kate quickened at his nearness. 'I'm fine,' she said lightly, defensively. 'Just hot . . .' She turned, smiling. But it was the kind of smile she might have bestowed on the merest acquaintance.

Her movement shifted his hand from her shoulder. Facing her, he rested both hands on the rail, one each side of her slender body, blocking her means of escape. Without even touching her, Kate felt he was much too close. He looked down at her with a smile in his eyes and her heart turned over at the charm of that too attractive face. Every fibre of her being was much too conscious of him.

She looked back at him steadily, determined not to betray the turmoil that he evoked. She clenched her hands to keep from putting them against his chest. With every intention of thrusting him further away, she might be too tempted to slide her hands up and about his neck instead.

'I thought you might need a doctor,' he said lightly,

eyes crinkling with amusement, slight relief. His smile was suddenly very warm, beguiling. 'I hoped you might even need *me*,' he added, very soft, meaningful.

Remembering how he had held the staff nurse, murmuring to her, smiling into her eyes, only minutes before, Kate hardened the heart that wanted too much to believe all that was in his coaxing words. She would not be flattered by anything he said or did, she rebelled. He was too unpredictable, too unreliable. He could have brought her to this party. Instead, he had brought Elinor Nicholls who was probably much more experienced than she was and knew just how to play the game of love that he obviously enjoyed so much.

It was not a game to Kate. In fact, it threatened to become so serious that she knew she had to keep him at a safe distance. He would surely soon give up, lose interest, retreat from the chase.

'No, thanks,' she retorted, equally light. 'I'm falling over doctors every day of the week!'

He laughed. 'All at your feet, of course!'

It was blatant flattery. She smiled as he had intended. Most of them are much too busy to notice me—and that's the way I like it,' she said firmly.

'But some do,' he said, very dryly 'Senior registrars, for instance—and even consultants. You aim high, Kate. No wonder you don't want to know a very ordinary houseman.' His hands dropped abruptly from the rail.

She saw the flicker of sudden anger cross his handsome face and wondered. She was puzzled by his words, by the seething resentment behind them. Obviously he referred to David Montgomery and she was tempted to believe that he was jealous of her apparent liking for the registrar. She did not understand the reference to consultants. Most of them were too old or too married to give her a second glance on the rare occasions that their paths crossed.

. She knew two or three through their association with her father, of course. Perhaps Todd had seen one of them smile in passing or pause briefly to ask how she was getting on at Hartlake. That kind of attention from a very senior doctor to a very junior nurse would obviously be remarked. But there was no reason why Todd should resent it so much. That hint of suppressed anger indicated that he did.

'Some of my best friends are housemen,' she said flippantly. 'I'm not a snob.'

The perfume of her hair was teasing his senses and the curve of the lovely breasts, the pale skin through the filmy blouse, excited him to swift, throbbing desire. More, his heart stirred as he looked down at the lovely face with its rare quality of innocence—so enchanting and so deceptive!

It seemed that she went readily into the arms of Sir Terence, thirty years older and much married. Todd had observed her warmly encouraging response to David Montgomery. He knew that she was on very friendly terms with a couple of the medical students. Why the devil did she keep *him* at arms' length so stubbornly?

'No. But you're a tease,' he said, a little angry. 'It's a dangerous game, Kate. A man may be tempted to take what you won't give for all the promising!'

Kate sensed the growing tension in him that was unmistakably sexual. Her own pulses throbbed at the sudden passion in his tone. She looked at him, seeing tautness in the lean jaw, the shadow of anger in his eyes.

He did not like to be thwarted, she knew. He was not used to rebuff. She should fall into his arms as apparently every other girl did! She suspected that it was only her refusal to do so that kept him in pursuit. If she was ever fool enough to give him what he wanted then she would deserve to be discarded and forgotten as soon as he tired, like all the others, she told herself sternly.

'That sounds like a threat,' she said, light but very cool, keeping a tight rein on the feelings that threatened to betray her into folly. 'I'll have to make sure that you never get a chance to carry it out!'

Todd's hands clenched against the impulse to seize her and shake her and storm her into surrender. How could she look at him with those cold eyes and speak to him with such cold lips when her lovely body was trembling like a leaf in the wind with the desire he knew that he stirred in her!

She tried to brush past him. He caught her by the hand, held it tightly. 'Where are you going?'

'Back to the party, of course!'

'Back to Montgomery?' he challenged.

Her chin tilted. 'Possibly.' Her bright eyes demanded to know if he didn't mean to return to Elinor Nicholls?

'Is that serious?' he demanded, brusquely.

'Is that your business?' she countered in swift rebuke.

'I'm making it my business. Tell me, Kate . . .' Put an end to hoping if not to wanting, his tone declared.

She hesitated. Then she said carefully: 'It could be.'

There was no likelihood of it for all the charm of the man, but she felt that she ought to cool Todd's almost frightening pursuit if she wanted to protect her heart and her pride. How better than by pretending more involvement with David than actually existed? And, without conceit, she knew it could become reality if she wished. For the good-looking registrar had already hinted that he wanted to see her again—and often.

'I see.'

Todd looked and sounded so grim that Kate was tempted to believe that he was really shaken by her liking for another man. Perhaps he was. It seemed that he was determined to have her if he could and another man must loom as an insurmountable obstacle.

Kate wondered why he wanted her so much when there were plenty of girls at Hartlake who would not be so cold, so discouraging. Just because she *was* cold and discouraging, probably. Reluctance and virginity—a combination that a man like Todd would certainly regard as an irresistible challenge, she thought dryly.

She was very conscious of his firm clasp. She ought to escape from him as quickly as she could, she knew. But he seemed to be holding her captive with far more than that grip on her hand. The potent magic of his attraction was casting its spell on her all over again.

'I—I like David . . . very much,' she said, the words tumbling over themselves in the effort to convince him that it was pointless to go on wanting her, pursuing her. 'And he—well, he cares about me. Really cares, I mean.' Her chin went up. 'It isn't just sex,' she said, defiant. 'He—he *respects* me!'

An old-fashioned word, she knew. But she was old-fashioned in her attitudes for all the permissiveness on all sides—and it wouldn't be a bad thing for Todd to realise it. She might like him better if he wasn't so eager to bed every girl in sight before sex went out of fashion!

Todd wondered if she was defying him or her own feelings. He felt her hand tremble in his clasp. The fact that she did not pull away from him told its own story, he felt. Whether she was prepared to admit it or not, she wanted him as much as he wanted her!

'And you think I don't?' he said quietly. 'You know better, Kate. I could have taken what I wanted the other night—and you know it! Or I could have talked you into bed with the kind of lies that come easily to some men. I've too much respect for all women for that kind of thing. Not just you!'

Rebuked, she was silent.

He looked down at her, thoughtful. 'So Montgomery cares about you? Wants to marry you, does he?'

Kate discovered that she had been a little too convincing. If she was not careful, it would be all over Hartlake that she was going to marry a man that she had only met for the first time that evening! David might not be too pleased about that!

'Oh, well—I mean . . . David is working for a consultancy,' she said hastily. 'And I want to finish training, get my badge. We—we haven't really talked too seriously about getting married . . .'

I bet you haven't, he thought, knowing his friend rather better than she obviously did. He scarcely knew whether to be amused or angry that she was fighting so hard to keep him at bay with a very transparent fabrication.

He did not doubt that they were friends, possibly lovers. But he did doubt if it was anything more than the usual light-hearted affair that David enjoyed so often, just as he did.

'And what does Sir Terence say to it?' he drawled. 'How does *he* feel about your not-quite engagement to Montgomery?' He might know that the whole thing was a myth. But it was an opportunity to bring into the open the shadow that really did stand between them, he thought.

'Oh, he doesn't know,' Kate declared, a little too quickly. He was making far too much of a foolish pretence that she already regretted, she thought impatiently. Now, lumbered with a lie, it seemed she must go on with it. 'No one does! And you won't mention it, will you?' she urged anxiously. 'Not to anyone, I mean . . . ?'

She would die of embarrassment if he talked about a relationship that did not even exist. And David would be justifiably furious!

Todd's eyes narrowed. The words seemed to be a confirmation he had not really needed of her involvement with the middle-aged consultant. It dismayed and puzzled him for he found it very hard to equate the innocence that shone from those lovely eyes with his knowledge of her illicit relationship with Sir Terence. He wondered how far she would go to protect that relationship.

'I won't queer your pitch if you make it worth my while,' he said lightly, testing her and not at all in earnest.

Kate stared. 'I don't know what you mean.'

'I take it that you don't want to upset Sir Terence?' he suggested.

She was still puzzled. 'Well, I don't know that it would upset him, exactly . . .' she began and then broke off, annoyed with herself for talking as though the ridiculous business of David Montgomery was *real*. 'What are you getting at, Todd?' she demanded.

'Darling, don't you recognise blackmail when you hear it?' he drawled, a little mischief dancing in his eyes. 'I won't mention anything to anyone—and in return . . . well, I don't have to spell it out, do I?' He smiled at her warmly. 'Fair means or foul, Kate!'

It took a moment or two to grasp his meaning. Then she was furious and very dismayed to discover that he would go to any dubious lengths to get what he wanted. It was absurd, of course. As if she would go to bed with him rather than have her parents find out about a non-existent affair with another man! The whole thing was so absurd that she should have known immediately that he could not be serious. But she was much too angry to think straight.

'You really are despicable,' she declared coldly, with contempt. She tugged her hand from his clasp and turned away with a flounce of her long skirt, feeling that she never wanted to see or speak to him again.

He spun her round with a hand on her shoulder, angry in his turn. 'Don't be an idiot, Kate! How can you think I mean it? You know me better than that, surely!'

'No, I don't!' She glared at him. 'I think you'd do anything to get a girl you want into bed! I should hate to be in a position where you really could blackmail me!'

His eyes narrowed. 'It was a joke,' he said quietly. 'In bad taste, perhaps—but a joke. When you cool down, you'll realise it. And if you are honest you'll admit that I

don't need to twist your arm, Kate. All I need is the
mood and the moment together—and that day will
dawn. I can wait.'

'You'll wait a very long time!' she told him fiercely.

'Will I, Kate?' Before she knew what he was about, he
caught her face in his hands and kissed her, hard and
urgent. Her mouth quivered beneath his own and he
sensed the leaping response in that slight body. He
released her, a little smile lurking about his lips. 'Something on account,' he said softly.

Her eyes flashed. 'Sometimes I don't even like you!'
she stormed—and brushed past him, head high and
heart thudding.

David welcomed her back with flattering warmth and
forbore to question her lengthy absence. If he noticed
that Todd followed her into the room almost immediately, carefully not looking in her direction, he did not say
so.

David was very good-looking, very personable and
obviously very interested in knowing her better. Kate
wondered why she felt so reluctant to push Todd out of
her life with both hands and concentrate on a man who
did not make it painfully obvious that his one aim in life
was to seduce her!

As far as she knew, David did not have that kind of
reputation and it would probably be a good idea to
encourage him, to go out with him, to enjoy a light-
hearted relationship with a little romancing to give it
spice. It was foolish to feel that she could not enjoy his
kisses just because she had quickened so rapturously to
that leaping fire in Todd's embrace, she told herself
firmly.

David was a clever and ambitious surgeon and it was a feather in her cap to have attracted his interest. He was exactly the kind of man that her parents would wish her to know and they would certainly welcome him into the family if she should fall in love and wish to marry him. It *was* possible, pride argued with her wilful heart.

She certainly did not mean to love Todd! He would never marry her! Only a fool would think it possible or want it to happen. A man like Todd would not find favour in her parents' eyes, she knew. For one thing, he was still in the early stages of his medical career and would probably become a very ordinary GP, overworked and underpaid. David was obviously destined to be a consultant. For another, her parents were very concerned for the welfare and happiness of their one ewe lamb—and Todd was the kind of wolf in wolf's clothing that they would instinctively mistrust, she thought dryly.

Kate did not trust him, either. He was too much of a threat to her heart, her virginity and her future as a Hartlake nurse!

Just now, she was furious with him. But she knew her anger would die away and she would forgive him. She was already cooling and beginning to accept that the absurd attempt at blackmail *had* been a joke, remembering the glint of mischief in his eyes and his genuine dismay that she had taken him seriously. At any other time she might have responded to that mischievous sense of humour and laughed with him. But she had been over-sensitive, too aware that she had set a trap for herself with foolish lies, suspecting that Todd knew she had lied—and just why!

Just now, she would not even smile at him when their

eyes met across the room. How dare he be so sure of himself—and of her! It would do him a great deal of good to realise that not every girl would come running at the lift of his finger, she told herself firmly—and hoped she would not weaken.

He left the party with the staff nurse and the evening fell completely flat for Kate, although she continued to smile on David Montgomery and even to flirt with him a little.

David took her back to the Nurses' Home in his car and kissed her goodnight in a gentle, undemanding way that still allowed her to know that he found her very attractive.

Unlike the Todd Morgans of this world, he did not mean to rush his fences with ardent kisses and urgent embrace, it seemed. Kate was grateful. She knew where she was with a man like David who would allow a relationship to develop at an acceptable pace. Todd had alarmed her with the urgency of his passion. It was even more alarming that she had been so responsive, so ready to throw all caution to the winds.

With David's cool lips on her own and his arm lightly about her shoulders, Kate refused to yearn for the kiss and the touch and the exciting embrace of a man who was probably making passionate love to the good-looking staff nurse at that very moment.

Resolutely, she kept her mind on David as she took off her clothes as quietly as possible in the room that she shared with the soundly sleeping Phyllida.

She had agreed to go out with David one evening and she told herself that she liked him and would enjoy his company, even if he wasn't the kind of man she could please her parents by loving and wishing to marry eventually. He might be all that a girl could want. Kate knew that she would never want him.

For Todd undeniably stirred her heart as well as her senses and she was very near to loving him, she thought wryly. Even if he was the kind of man that no girl ought to love at all!

CHAPTER SEVEN

THE heat-wave continued—and so did the accidents. A toddler nearly drowned in the local paddling-pool. Cyclists skidded on roads made treacherous by a combination of heat and rubber from car wheels. There were cases of heat exhaustion in the elderly who wore several layers of clothing come winter or summer. Sunbathers arrived with scorched and blistered bodies because they wore too few clothes in the blazing sun.

Despite the frantic pace on A and E, Kate found time to look and listen for Todd. Her heart could bound at the merest whisk of a white coat below a dark head, she discovered to her dismay.

Kate was glad that she hadn't taken him seriously. She reminded herself that she didn't really like him and decided that it was a relief to be free of the feeling that she might yield to the undeniable lure of his physical magnetism.

She was not expecting to see him as she came out of a cubicle where Sister and a doctor were busy with a man brought in with severe abdominal pain and haemorrhaging from the mouth. He was going directly to Theatres, but his veins were so collapsed that it had been necessary to tie a cannula into position to ensure a route for saline, plasma or whole blood if necessary.

Todd came thrusting through the swing doors with a

small boy in his arms, followed by a young and very earnest policeman with notebook at the ready. The child's fair hair was blood-stained and matted to his head and he was very pale. Todd's blue shirt was smeared with blood and oil and he looked grim. Kate hurried towards him, forgetting to notice the leap of her foolish heart.

'Caught him with my car,' Todd said brusquely. 'He was running out after an ice-cream van . . .' He took the boy into a cubicle and laid him gently on the couch while Kate hurried for a trolley, laid-up in readiness for this kind of emergency. On the way back, she smiled at the hovering policeman and suggested he should take a seat until the doctor was free to talk to him.

She drew the curtains around the couch and turned to assist. 'Why, it's Shane!' she exclaimed, suddenly recognising the accident-prone youngster who seemed destined to make a rather longer stay than usual. His eyes were closed and he winced as Todd's gentle hands ran over him in skilled examination, but Kate saw that he still clutched some money in a small, grubby hand. 'Is he badly hurt?'

'Fracture of the left tibia, I think. Certainly a couple of broken ribs and some internal bruising, but no serious damage, I imagine. Head and chest X-rays as well as all limbs, of course. Cleaned and stitched, that gash in the head is probably not as bad as it looks just now.' He bent over the boy who was tight-lipped with the stoicism for which he was noted. 'All right, lad . . . hurts, does it? I'll give you something for it very soon.'

'Didn't get me ice-cream,' Shane said with obvious resentment.

Todd grinned. 'Never mind. I'll tell Sister to put it on

the menu every day. You'll be staying with us for a few days.'

'What about me Mum?'

'She'll be told. Don't worry.' He patted the boy's shoulder. 'She's used to seeing a policeman on her doorstep with that kind of news, isn't she? You're one of our regular customers.'

'Your bleeding fault this time!'

Todd raised an eyebrow. 'You dashed into the road, son.' He turned to Kate. 'The kind of witness who'd put me behind bars,' he murmured dryly. 'Clean him up a bit, Nurse—and I'll have a word with Sister about X-rays and admission.'

He strode away. Later, Kate saw him talking to the policeman who seemed satisfied with his version of the accident and went away after entering the details in his notebook.

She took Shane to X-ray and then to the Plaster Room and eventually accompanied him to the children's ward where he was greeted without surprise by Sister. She went back to A and E, feeling just a little vexed that Todd had been so offhand. He might have granted her one special smile, one meaningful glance, even if he had been shaken by that encounter with the boy.

It seemed that he had very little time for her, after all. He had behaved as though she was a stranger. Well, Elinor Nicholls was welcome to him! For herself, there was no shortage of men who liked her and sought her company and did not make her feel that sex was the only thing on their minds.

David Montgomery, for one . . .

Kate could not help comparing the evening she spent

with David to that evening with Todd. It was hard to imagine anything going wrong for David. He was so capable, so well organised. He took her to the theatre, too. Traffic miraculously melted before the sleek Mercedes and a parking space appeared promptly on cue as he drew up opposite the theatre. There was plenty of time for drinks before the show. Seated in the best stalls, an expensive box of sweets in her lap and an attentive man at her side, knowing that she was looking her very best, Kate had every reason to enjoy the sophisticated revue that was as successful in its own way as Todd's musical.

Certainly there was no reason at all why her thoughts should turn so frequently to a very different evening and a very different man.

After the show, David took her to the Ivy, a favourite eating-place of theatricals. Kate was fascinated to recognise so many celebrities and it seemed that David knew many of them. His mother was an actress and backstage was as familiar to him as his home. All his family had greasepaint in their blood but he had no talent for acting and so had settled for a different kind of theatre, he explained.

'There is a similarity,' he added lightly. 'A hospital deals in tragedy and comedy and even kitchen-sink drama at times. The cast is enormous and constantly changing. We have our successes and our failures, just as they do in show business. We have to be as highly trained and as disciplined as any member of the theatrical profession. The real difference lies in the fact that they portray life and we actually deal with it—*and* death, too often.'

Kate smiled at him. She had enjoyed the show, the meal, his company. She liked his light touch. She didn't doubt his admiration, his interest, his wish to know more of her in the days to come. But there was no hint of pressure. Unlike Todd, he was the kind to let things take their steady course towards a more meaningful relationship, she felt. Unlike Todd, he was not only concerned with whisking her into bed before moving on to the next conquest, she thought, a trifle bitterly. He was nice, thoughtful, obviously reliable. Kate carefully avoided the thought that he was just a little unexciting.

She could relax in his company. She didn't need to be constantly on her guard against an insidious and dangerous excitement. She could look forward to a comfortable relationship with the good-looking registrar that might one day slip naturally into loving. Maybe one day if Todd or anyone else asked her if it was a serious affair, she would answer with truth that she hoped to marry David Montgomery . . .

It was further evidence of his consideration that he returned her in good time to the Nurses' Home. There was no need for climbing through windows or hoping that a friend would be on hand to let her in! Kissing her in his car, his lips lingered on her own with rather more warmth than she had expected and she felt the tentative touch of his hand at her breast. Quite unable to help it, she stiffened and her hand flew to check the caress. He smiled into her eyes without the least resentment, sliding his hand to her waist. Todd would have persisted, she felt—but that was Todd!

David kissed her again, very lightly. Grateful for his undemanding niceness, Kate allowed her lips to soften

See over for details

Fall in love with Mills & Boon

Do you remember the first time you fell in love? The heart-ache, the excitement, the happiness?

Mills & Boon know–that's why they're the best-loved name in romantic fiction. The world's finest romance authors bring to life the emotions, the conflicts and the joys of true love, and you can share them– between the covers of a Mills & Boon.

Accept 6 books FREE

Postage will be paid by Mills & Boon

Do not affix Postage Stamps if posted in Gt. Britain, Channel Islands, N. Ireland or the Isle of Man

BUSINESS REPLY SERVICE
Licence No CN81

Mills & Boon Reader Service,
PO Box 236,
CROYDON,
Surrey CR9 9EL.

2

Now you can enjoy all 12 latest Mills & Boon Romances every month. As a subscriber to our Reader Service, you'll receive all our new titles, delivered to your doorstep—postage and packing Free. There's no commitment—you can change your mind about subscribing at any time, but the 6 free books are yours to keep.

Take Six Books FREE!

That's right! Return the coupon now and your first parcel of books is absolutely Free. There are lots of other advantages—no hidden extra charges, a free monthly Newsletter, and our famous friendly service—'phone our editor Susan Welland now on 01-684 2141 if you have any queries.

You have nothing to lose—and a whole new world of Romance to gain. Fill in and post the coupon today—and send no money!

NO STAMP NEEDED

To: Mills & Boon Reader Service,
PO Box 236, Croydon, Surrey CR9 9EL.

Please send me, *free and without obligation,* six of the latest Mills & Boon Romances, and reserve a Reader Service Subscription for me. If I decide to subscribe, I shall, from the beginning of the month following my free parcel of books, receive 12 new books each month for £10.20, post and packing free. If I decide not to subscribe, I shall write to you within 21 days *but whatever I decide the free books are mine to keep.* I understand that I may cancel my subscription at any time simply by writing to you. I am over 18 years of age.

Please write in BLOCK CAPITALS.

Name _____

Address _____

_____

_____ Post Code _____

Offer applies in the UK only. Overseas send for details.

SEND NO MONEY—TAKE NO RISKS 7D2A

and warm slightly. His arm tightened, but only enough to flatter and not to alarm.

She drew away from him, smiling. 'It's been a lovely evening, David.'

'We must do it again,' he said promptly.

She nodded. 'I'd like that . . .'

But they parted without a definite arrangement to meet. Kate knew he would be in touch when he was sure of his duty hours. It was a comforting kind of confidence in a man's interest, she felt, thinking of Todd's casual and cavalier attitude. He was such an arrogant devil in the way he assumed that he could take up a girl and drop her and take her up again as and when it suited him! It must be quite dreadful for any girl who wanted him so much that she was prepared to put up with such treatment. Kate did not—and would not!

But that resolution weakened all in a moment when they met later in the week . . .

Todd was a keen squash player. He liked to keep fit and the game was an excellent way to relieve tension after a long day with the heavy responsibilities and many demands that made up a senior houseman's lot. A game of squash, a refreshing shower and a quiet drink in the club bar was a welcome change from chasing girls.

So girls—and even Kate—were far from his mind as he relaxed, ice-cold lager in his hand, only half-listening to a long and very complicated story that Roger Pelling was relating.

The administration wing was a modern block that contained not only offices but also a ballroom used for a variety of functions, the staff swimming pool and library, indoor squash and tennis courts and the social club that staff were encouraged to join, although the anti-social hours meant that they could not always make full use of the amenities. And, very often, staff did not choose to spend their leisure hours in such close proximity to their work.

Kate preferred the club to the pub that was a favourite haunt for Hartlake staff. There was always someone she knew in the club and she could settle for tea or coffee or a soft drink if she didn't fancy anything stronger. There were a variety of things to do, too—table-tennis, darts, pool and sometimes a card game. Every Saturday there was a disco. Kate liked to dance.

Despite the heat and the noise and the flashing lights, she was enjoying the evening. She was young. She was pretty and popular and it was impossible not to know it as she laughed and talked and danced with a number of young men. For the first time in days, she was not thinking about Todd Morgan and it was a relief to discover that the man was not as important as she had begun to fear.

The disco was in a hall that adjoined the spacious bar lounge. Every time that the doors opened, Todd's ears were assailed by the music and the hubbub of voices. He was much too comfortable to move to a further corner. It was second nature for him to glance over the girls who went in or out in their off-duty clothes. Most of them were pretty. Some of them gave him back look for look with coquetry in eyes and smile. Todd's slow smile held a deal of promise, but he was too lazy to follow through— or getting old, he thought wryly.

It had been a hectic week and this was his first free evening for days. He did not think he wanted to spend what was left of it in getting to know yet another girl. A man began to tire of the eternal chase and wonder if there wasn't something to be said for settling for one girl at a time. As David did. It was rumoured that he was thinking of settling for Kate this time—and that had not improved Todd's mood when Roger told him.

Roger was called away to an emergency, being duty registrar that evening. Todd sat on, enjoying the cold beer, the solitude and the opportunity to look at the girls without feeling the need to pursue any of them.

He was surprised to see Kate in a cotton skirt and the kind of blouse that clung provocatively and revealingly to the small, tilting breasts. She wore nothing beneath it and his body stirred. She was enchantingly youthful with her soft hair falling about her face, eyes sparkling. Flushed and animated, she looked back over her shoulder with a smile for someone and Todd felt his heart contract with longing and a little jealousy.

Letting the door swing behind her, Kate crossed the big room, passing within feet of him. Todd knew that she had not noticed him. He watched as she was served with a pineapple juice and remained at the bar, drinking and talking to some friends. Then, her drink finished, she left the couple and walked over to the long window that opened on to a small paved area bordering the hospital garden.

She had obviously left the disco to cool down and get her breath back and it was typical of the independent Kate that she had bought her own drink, Todd thought, amused. He rose and made his way across to speak to her.

Kate stood just inside the window, glad of the breeze

that cooled her body through the thin blouse. It was really much too hot for anything as energetic as disco dancing and she was grateful for a brief respite.

She turned, startled, at the sound of her name in Todd's unmistakable deep voice. 'I didn't see you,' she said foolishly, defensively, and wondered why the heart that had leaped sky-high had not warned her in advance of his presence.

'And I haven't seen you for too long,' he returned smoothly. 'How are you, Kate?'

'I'm fine.' Her chin tilted. If he had not seen her, then that was his fault. Did he expect her to run after him? It still rankled that he had virtually ignored her in A and E the other day. A friendly word or a smile wouldn't have cost him anything.

Todd regarded her thoughtfully, remembering their encounter when she had evidently not been very pleased that he knew of her association with Sir Terence. He wondered if she had accepted that he would never stoop to using that knowledge to his own ends. 'You haven't forgiven me yet,' he said lightly.

Kate was briefly puzzled. Then she remembered. Refusing to be charmed by the warmth in his eyes, she said tartly: 'I haven't thought about you!' But her heart bumped and she was much too conscious of the thin blouse that had seemed so right for a disco on a hot night. She felt as if he saw right through the filmy material to the taut curves of her naked breasts.

He shook his head at her in reproach, eyes twinkling. A little colour came into her face. 'I've thought about you,' he told her. He took her arm and drew her out to the patio so that they were not observed. 'I promised not to pressure you,' he said quietly. 'Well, I haven't. It doesn't mean that I don't want you. I do. I need you, Kate.'

Slightly shocked by the blunt avowal of desire, Kate was torn between stirring excitement and instinctive dislike that any man should regard her as an object for sexual satisfaction. *I want you*, he said. *I need you.* He would probably never say that he loved her. Todd was governed by his senses rather than his heart. It hurt to realise all over again that she might never be anything more than another name on the long list of his casual and meaningless affairs if she yielded.

Silent, intent on resisting the persuasion and the passion in him and her own reluctant response to another of his unexpected and entirely unpredictable overtures, she scarcely noticed the grip of his strong fingers on her slender wrist.

'Don't you think my patience deserves some small reward? You could admit to being glad to see me, for instance?' he coaxed, gently mocking.

'I'm not!'

Todd had her pulse beneath his fingers and could feel its frantic fluttering. He saw the quickened rise and fall of the lovely breasts. He saw the heartbeat in the hollow of her throat and the little tremor of her lips. He recognised it as a touchingly defensive lie.

He was aching to kiss her, to sweep her into his arms. With his lips on her own, her body crushed against him, could Kate then deny that she was consumed with the flame that leaped to life between them when they touched?

No, but she probably would, he thought wryly. This

girl was so proud, so determined not to lie in his arms and be loved. He wondered if the moment would ever be right for him. She seemed to give so generously to everyone else!

Kate knew before he bent his dark head that he meant to kiss her. Whether she liked it or not! He was that kind of man. She instantly determined that she would not kiss him!

He touched his lips to the soft, hesitant mouth. He heard the catch of her breath and sensed the stubborn resistance in that slender body. He wanted to compel her to the swift and eager response that had so enchanted and delighted him before. But this was not the mood or the moment, he thought wryly.

'One kiss won't cost you anything,' he said, against the cold lips, gently reproaching. 'Give a little, girl . . .'

Kate refused to be seduced by that coaxing tone or the pressure of his warm body into giving anything at all. One kiss would only lead to another and she did not trust that tingling in her veins or the foolish lift of her heart.

His lips moved to the corner of her mouth, her soft cheek. He nuzzled the lobe of her ear. His kiss trailed a route via the slender lines of her neck to the warm curve of her breast, his lips burning through the flimsy cotton.

A shudder rippled along her spine. Kate could hardly breathe for the pounding of her heart, the wave of desire that swept over her.

Abruptly he put his arms about her and drew her against him, pressing his cheek to her soft hair. 'Kate, I want you so much,' he said, low, urgent. 'More than any woman I've ever known . . .'

She was flooded with painful disappointment, sick

dismay. For everything about that embrace spoke of sexual wanting, sexual need. There was not the least hint of loving. She could not be unmoved by the passion that trembled in his tone, in his lean, taut body. It echoed the tumult of her own. But the way she felt about him was more than merely physical.

She pushed him away. 'I wish you'd stop bothering me, Todd,' she said impatiently. 'Why don't you know when you're not wanted!'

Angry with herself for being so weak where he was concerned, she was more convincing than she meant to be. She saw the sudden narrowing of his eyes, the sudden tightening of his mouth. It was tempting to wonder if he cared more than he was prepared to admit.

'Well, I know now, don't I?' he said quietly, a nerve jumping in his cheek.

Kate felt a little panic. Had she been too tart, too snubbing? She did not really want to lose his interest so completely. It was only that she was frightened of giving too much—and now she was frightened that she had not given enough to hold a man who could get what he wanted from any woman.

'I didn't mean that, exactly,' she said quickly, lamely.

Todd looked at her steadily. 'Do you know, I think that's exactly what you did mean,' he drawled. 'Let's leave it at that, shall we . . .?' He turned away.

Kate felt a little contraction of her heart. She had the oddest conviction that she had hurt him quite badly and that she would not get the chance to do it again.

'Todd . . . !' His name leapt to her lips before she could check the impulse.

He paused, looked back—and then stepped through

the window to join her on the patio. 'What is it?' he asked, brusquely.

Impulse had carried her so far. Now shy confusion took over. She was only nineteen and trembling on the threshold of loving.

Todd looked down at her, waiting, an eyebrow quirked in query and no trace of a smile in those compelling blue eyes.

Kate felt foolish. He knew just why she had called him back, she suspected—and he did not mean to help her out!

She shook her head. 'It doesn't matter. My friends will be wondering where I am . . .' She tried to brush past him. He blocked the way.

'Are you with Montgomery?'

'No.' She was startled by the abrupt, almost angry question.

Todd relaxed. 'Good. You're seeing too much of him,' he said lightly and smiled as her eyes widened in sudden outrage. 'Sir Terence wouldn't like it—and neither do I.'

'You've no say in the matter,' Kate told him swiftly, with spirit.

'Only because you're so stubborn,' he returned smoothly. 'Why won't you let me get near to you, Kate? What are you fighting, for heaven's sake?'

She bit her lip. How could she tell him that she was fighting the foolish readiness of her heart to love him? But it would be dreadful to lose her heart to a man who was urgent to possess only her body and Kate did not think that she could bear to enjoy only a brief happiness with him and then suffer the heartache and humiliation of being discarded for someone else. It hurt enough now to know that he took his sexual satisfaction with other girls while she kept him resolutely at a distance.

'Darling . . .' he said gently and touched his fingers to her cheek in a little caress.

Her heart trembled. If only he meant the tenderness and the longing that was in the meaningful but meaningless word.

Her smile was shaky. But it was a smile—and Todd was encouraged. They progressed, he thought, slowly but it was progress!

Even if she did back away and turn into the lounge and hurry across to return to her friends in the disco. Todd knew she was running from her own feelings rather than from anything he had said or done.

CHAPTER EIGHT

As THE small, broken body of a child who had been injured in a road accident was hurried to the Intensive Care Unit, Sister Carmichael sent Kate to tidy the cubicle where he had been examined and get it ready for the next patient.

She was washing the couch with a strong solution of disinfectant when Todd came into the cubicle and whisked the curtains across to screen them from the interested gaze of patients sitting on the rows of benches, waiting for attention.

'I'm busy!' Kate said hastily, not very pleased to see him when her cap was steadily sliding over one ear, her apron was in a dreadful state and she was up to her elbows in hot water. 'Go away!'

He stood his ground, watching her work, hands in the pockets of his white coat. 'When can I see you?'

'You can't!' she retorted, chin lifting.

But her heart lifted, too. For he must like her a lot to keep coming back despite all the snubs, she thought, a little comforted after a restless night of troubled dreams in which he had gone out of her life for good.

'Tonight?'

'No! Go away and let me get on. Sister isn't in a very good mood this morning and we're so busy.' She brushed the heavy fall of hair from her forehead with a wet hand, a soft flush in her cheeks, carefully not meeting his eyes.

Todd looked down at her thoughtfully. The guarded expression in those lovely eyes grieved even while it encouraged him. What was she so afraid he might read in their depths?

'Tomorrow night?'

'I have a date.'

But she was weakening and they both knew it. She was too conscious of him in that confined space, tall and impressive and much too attractive, melting her very bones with his sudden smile.

'Tonight then, Kate.'

He was urgent, compelling, and her heart gave a flutter of alarm at his intensity. She wished she could believe that it came from a real and lasting need that she could trust and welcome. Instead, she knew it was only frustrated desire and an insistence on getting what he wanted that throbbed in his deep voice.

He saw the flicker of distrust that crossed her face. His hands clenched in his pockets but he said quietly, carefully: 'You said that I rushed you. I won't make that mistake again. I won't even kiss you unless you want it. That's a promise. We meet for a drink and a friendly chat. Where's the harm in that?'

Kate looked at him doubtfully. But she was disarmed by the sincerity and the warm persuasion of the words. It might be possible to trust him. But could she trust the way she felt about him? Meeting those incredibly blue eyes with that disturbing glow in their depths, Kate wondered wryly if she could trust herself to deny him anything at all.

Todd was as proud as he was passionate and it was becoming increasingly hard for her to hold out against the insidious flattery of that seeming readiness to swallow his pride again and again for her sake. She was a woman like any other—and she was desperately afraid that he would abruptly give up, turn away, finally dismiss her. If that happened, she would have missed out on the most wonderful experience of her life, she thought in a little panic.

Common-sense declared that she would lose him almost as soon as she melted into his arms. The chase and the conquest were all that mattered to a man like Todd. Instinct reached out with eager yearning for the promise in his kiss, his touch, his strong arms. He had given her a brief glimpse of the heaven to be found with him. She might never know it with any other man.

Before she could answer him, Sister Carmichael's voice was clearly heard as she ushered a patient into the adjoining cubicle with cheerful, practised reassurances. Kate felt sure that at any moment the curtains would be pulled back to expose her in tête-a-tête with Todd who really had no business to be in A and E—and that would certainly mean a visit to Matron's office!

Seeing the hint of alarm in those grey eyes, Todd took swift advantage of a junior nurse's natural reluctance to fall foul of authority.

'Tonight,' he said again, softly in her ear, and it was not a request. 'Nine o'clock in the Kingfisher.'

He was gone before Kate could murmur yea or nay. But she knew that she would meet him.

Sister Carmichael, emerging from the next cubicle,

looked after the swiftly retreating back of the houseman. She glanced through the partly-drawn curtains at the junior who was scrubbing at the couch as though her life depended on it, rather flushed.

She checked the sarcastic comment that flew to her lips. The girl worked hard and she promised to be a good and caring nurse and a little harmless flirtation in the midst of a busy day could soften the harshness and tension of work on A and E. Accident cases could be upsetting for juniors like Nurse Murray, new to nursing. Heaven knew it was no picnic for experienced staff who had to deal with emergencies from a multiple car crash, brought in more dead than alive and dreadfully mangled in some cases.

The girl had obviously been distressed by the condition of the child who had a ruptured spleen and a punctured lung and probable bruising of the cerebral cortex and was in coma, unlikely to live for all the efforts of the Intensive Care Unit. A few stolen moments with an attractive doctor had probably made the junior feel better, Sister Carmichael decided tolerantly, being more human than anyone suspected.

The day dragged on leaden feet for Kate despite all the pressure of work. The spell of hot weather had ended abruptly with a severe thunderstorm in the night and torrential rain had been falling for most of the day. They dealt in A and E with a crop of motor-cyclists with fortunately minor injuries for the most part. An elderly man was brought in with a fractured skull, having slipped on the wet pavement and hit his head on the kerb. An ancient and very smelly tramp collapsed in the street and arrived in A and E, more drunk than dying, and was duly admitted to a ward for treatment for a chest infection.

The rows of patients did not seem to diminish. Kate bustled between X-ray and Theatres and Path Lab and Dispensary and various wards. She soothed frightened children and reassured harassed mothers and coped with men who demanded instant treatment for minor lacerations and bruises or nosebleeds before getting back to work. She tidied cubicles and laid up trolleys and sterilised instruments and handed surgical packs or syringes or hypodermics and ampules to sister or staff nurse or a casualty officer. She held a screaming child while a doctor gave an injection and comforted another who was being persistently sick and hurried with a newly-born and very premature baby to a waiting incubator and then sped with it to the Baby Unit.

During that seemingly endless day, Kate coaxed and cajoled and comforted, mopped up blood and vomit and spilled urine, helped a dozen patients with dressing or undressing, changed her apron several times and finally went off duty wondering why on earth she had ever wanted to be a nurse.

Her feet ached, her back ached and she was longing for a hot bath, a meal and a very early night. Even to meet Todd, she doubted if she would be able to drag herself to the Kingfisher later that night!

Wrapped in her cape, Kate pushed open the glass doors that led to the street from Main Hall, having managed a smile for Jimmy who never seemed to go off duty. She paused at the head of the stone steps. It was still raining heavily and a brisk wind scurried the raindrops along the pavements and whipped them spitefully into the faces of hurrying, huddled pedestrians in the High Street. It was surprisingly cold, too. Winter was back with a vengeance after the summery days of early May. The pessimists declared that it was all the summer they were likely to get!

Kate was sagging with weariness and her head and heart were filled with the sights and sounds and strains of the day. Sunday was the busiest day of the week for Accident and Emergency—everyone else's day of rest!

She hoped she had the stamina to survive her training. Three years of hard work, long hours and tough discipline were enough to test any girl's vocation for the job. A nurse had to be brisk and efficient and capable, steady of hand and strong of stomach. She had to be too concerned for the patient to notice the unpleasant state of his condition at times. She must never, never let a patient know that she was dismayed or frightened or repelled or that she did not know exactly what to do to ease his pain and alleviate his anxiety. Injured or ill, shocked or apprehensive, a patient always expected a nurse, however junior, to comfort and reassure and tend him with experienced hands. If she did not know what to do—and that frequently happened in Kate's case—then she brought someone who did and watched carefully, observing and remembering, in readiness for the next occasion.

So much was expected from them that it was no wonder they were referred to as angels, Kate thought wryly. No one really expected a nurse to be human, after all. On duty, she must smile in the face of all odds while she worked until she nearly dropped. She must put up with difficult and demanding and sometimes abusive patients who always assumed that their case was unique in medical history and that every detail was fresh in the mind of every member of staff. She must listen meekly to lectures and scolds from bossy seniors and scurry hither and thither at their bidding. She must bury her nose in books and cram her brain with a thousand facts to prepare for the dreaded exams when she was so tired that she only wanted to crawl into bed.

A nurse had to be much tougher than she usually looked, too. Because of her delicate colouring and bone structure, Kate looked as fragile as a lovely flower. But she was young and healthy, brimming with energy and enthusiasm—and, most important of all, she really loved nursing.

She liked people and she had a warm heart that went out to the sick and old and disabled. Her concern was more practical than sentimental and so she had become a nurse. At the moment, she was just a much-needed pair of hands, obedient and willing. But in time she would prove to her own satisfaction at least that she was a good nurse, she told herself, straightening her back and chiding herself for looking less than cheerful and efficient as the never-ending stream of people mounted the steps to the main entrance of the hospital, glancing at her curiously as they passed. Some of them smiled, nodded, spoke a courteous greeting as if they knew her. All nurses looked alike, she had discovered. They were faceless angels to a grateful public.

Kate did not mind. She liked to feel that she was recognised and accepted, not as an individual, but as a member of a profession that had been valued and respected since the days of Florence Nightingale. It made her feel less new and inexperienced, less of a liability to overworked senior staff. It made her feel that she really was a nurse, after all!

Spirits lifting, no longer feeling quite so tired and jaded, Kate hurried along the High Street towards the Nurses' Home in the drenching rain.

Phyllida and Patti were working on the wards until late. Only Jacqui was in the flat, making herself a snack of eggs on toast. The fragrant aroma of coffee greeted Kate as she entered and she sniffed appreciatively. Jacqui reached for another mug, smiling at her.

Kate fell into a chair and eased off the neat black brogues that were regulation wear with her uniform. She pulled off her cap and tossed it carelessly into a corner. 'What a day!' she sighed.

'Meaning the weather or the work?' Jacqui handed her a mug of coffee. She was a slender, fair girl with long hair that she wore knotted on the nape of her neck. She was a gentle dreamer who did not seem very suited to the practical demands of nursing and she spent more time studying than most of her set. Shy and apparently unaware that she was pretty, she avoided much of the social whirl that her flatmates regarded as a necessary antidote to long hours and hard work on the wards.

'Both!' Kate said with feeling, both hands wrapped gratefully about the mug of steaming coffee.

Jacqui picked up her damp cape and took it into the tiny bathroom, hanging it up to dry. It was done so naturally and unobtrusively that Kate did not feel reproached although she knew that she ought not to let her friend wait on her. No doubt Jacqui's day had been just as long and just as hard. Kate complained long and often, cheerfully letting off steam at the end of a busy and demanding day. So did Phyllida. But Jacqui, like Patti, never seemed to mind anything—aching feet, menial tasks, bossy seniors, demanding patients or the difficulty of enjoying a normal social life between irregular hours of duty and the insistence of Sister Tutor that they should spend most of their free time in study.

Jacqui's books and papers were already out in readiness for the evening's work. Kate thought of her own, bundled into a cupboard and silently reproaching her with neglect. She ought not to meet Todd that evening. She really should devote a few hours to studying and it was scarcely a night to tempt anyone out of doors.

But it would be warm and bright and very cheerful in the pub—and she could always rely on Todd to teach her a little anatomy, she thought dryly, a smile hovering. He would be more exciting than her books, anyway—and they would still be around long after he had slipped out of her life as he inevitably would. Kate faced the fact squarely—and knew she must make the most of what offered while he was still interested. Even at the risk of the heartache to come . . .

It was not an evening for dressing up but Kate liked to change out of uniform when she was off duty, like most nurses. It was nice to feel like a woman instead of the efficient robot that most doctors and every patient expected her to be! She put on one of her prettiest frocks for Todd.

The Kingfisher was crowded. Kate looked around for Todd, heart beating high in her throat. It was a few minutes to nine and no sign of him. She was too early, of course, betraying her eagerness.

Someone touched her shoulder and she swung round, a smile leaping swiftly to her eyes. She tried not to show that she was disappointed and slightly dismayed that it was not Todd but David. She smiled at him, warm enough to be friendly but not so warm that he could be misled, encouraged. 'Hallo, David.'

'On your own or meeting someone?'

'Meeting a friend.' She did not know why she was reluctant to mention Todd by name. Meeting him in a public place like the Kingfisher in full view of so many Hartlake staff certainly meant that everyone would soon know that he was trying for yet another conquest. She glanced at the big clock on the wall. 'I'm a little early . . .'

'He isn't here?' It didn't occur to David that she might be meeting a girl-friend. Girls as lovely as Kate did not need to spend their evenings in the company of their own sex. 'Let me get you a drink while you're waiting.' With a confident arm about her slender waist, he drew her towards the bar.

Kate was reluctant, but she felt that he was too nice to snub. She liked him and already thought of him as a friend. There was really no reason why she shouldn't have a drink with him—and Todd *was* late. Not on time, anyway, she amended as the clock chimed the hour.

It wasn't always easy for a doctor to get away from the wards promptly at the end of his working day. One had to make allowances. But Todd could be half an hour late if he was kept by an emergency and she could not sit in a crowded pub on her own, inviting all manner of doubtful attention from some of the unruly elements that abounded in the district. It was much better to sit with

David while she waited—and it was really rather lucky that he was in the pub that evening . . .

Todd was ten minutes late, delayed by a last-minute admission. He did not immediately see Kate, her slight figure blocked by the tall frame of his friend. His gaze slid over David's familiar back. He looked around, frowning slightly. He had only half-expected Kate to meet him that evening. She had a great deal of spirit and she was resisting him with all her might. His heart sank as he failed to find her in the crowded bar.

He turned at a touch on his arm, a smile in his blue eyes, her name already on his lips with warm, pleased delight. But it was not Kate and he stifled the exclamation of her name.

Elinor wondered at the expectation in his eyes and the instant disappointment, so ill-concealed. She smiled at him with her usual warmth. 'Looking for me, darling?' she asked lightly, knowing that she had been far from his mind.

It would be interesting to know which girl had briefly caught his fancy this time, she thought, not at all jealous. She did not love Todd in the least—and was thankful for it. She knew him well enough to doubt whether he knew the meaning of love. But he was an attractive and sensual man, a skilful and sensitive lover—and it amused Elinor to rekindle the fire in old flames from time to time.

'Hallo, Nell.' He smiled absently, his gaze still roving about the big room. 'Looking for a friend, actually . . .'

'I'm a friend,' she said, smiling. 'Will I do . . . ?' Something in eyes and voice reminded him that they had been more than friends on several occasions.

Todd turned to her, eyes crinkling with warm amusement. He did not feel guilty. She cared as little for him as he cared for her—and she knew the rules of the game better than many girls. He could rely on her not to make too much of a casual encounter or to make demands on him or to show any jealousy of his light-hearted pursuit of other women.

'Not tonight, Josephine,' he said, eyes dancing. 'I have to share it out, you know. So many girls and so little time . . .' He heaved a mock sigh.

Elinor laughed softly, affectionately. She was very close to him, warmth in her eyes and invitation in every line of her slender body. Kate, craning round David to look at the door in the hope that Todd would walk in, saw them together and felt their obvious intimacy like a physical blow.

He had stood her up! He had deliberately brought another girl into the pub where she was waiting for him—and that girl of all people! It was a slap in the face that she would never forgive! How could he! How dare he! What was he trying to do to her pride?

Todd saw Kate at the same moment, sitting with David Montgomery, a drink in her hand and a little eagerness about her manner that implied she was enjoying herself. It seemed she had chosen to spend her evening with the registrar rather than meet him. She had stood him up, he thought grimly. She had deliberately come into the Kingfisher with another man to show him how little she thought and felt for him! It was an unmistakable slap in the face!

Their eyes met. Neither smiled. Hurt and dismay trembled behind a mask of indifference worn to protect the pride. Kate looked through him, coldly. He looked back at her, stony.

Kate turned to David and smiled, spoke—not even knowing what she said for the dreadful pain that welled somewhere in the region of her heart and swept over her in waves, drowning her in despair.

Dismay, humiliation, anger, a terrible sense of loss— she did not know what she felt! But she did know that she never wanted to see or speak to Todd Morgan again— ever!

She had been a fool to like him, to feel that she could trust him, to have come so near to falling in love with him. Thank heavens she had realised his arrogance and his appalling contempt for her sex that outweighed all the charm and the physical attractions of the man! Thank heavens that in her short-lived dealings with him she had kept not only her head but her heart, too! Thank heavens it did not make a scrap of difference whether he was in her life or out of it!

Feeling that something very precious and very wonderful and very promising had suddenly been shattered beyond repair, Kate smiled and spoke to the unsuspecting David as though she did not have a care in the world.

Watching, Todd's mouth tightened and his hands balled into angry fists. He was consumed with the impulse to rush over to the bar, punch David's jaw for him and whisk Kate away from the man who seemed more important to her than a date with him. It might not solve anything. But it would certainly make him feel very much better, he thought grimly—and wondered if anything could!

He had never been so angry in his life. He had never been so bitterly disappointed in anyone. He had never wanted any woman so much that it was the end of his world because she did not want him at all—until now.

He turned to Elinor.

'On second thoughts . . . ' he said, forcing lightness into his tone. 'Why should I turn down the best offer I've had this evening?' He put an arm about her shoulders and smiled down at her just as though he was not filled with a black despair. 'I think you're just what I need, Nell,' he added, meaning it.

She did not blow hot and cold. She did not take his heart and twist it with smiling come-on and icy rebuff in turns. A man knew where he was with the warm-hearted staff nurse, a good friend in times of need. He had never needed her quite so much, he thought heavily.

In her arms, he ought to be able to blot out the memory of a lovely, flower-like face of a girl whose deceptive air of innocence and integrity had almost lured him into loving.

CHAPTER NINE

WHEN Kate looked again, there was no sign of Todd at all. Perhaps he was merely hidden from her view by others or perhaps he had taken the staff nurse through to the other, slightly less crowded, bar. She did not want to think that they might have left the pub for more intimate surroundings.

He seemed to be very involved with the attractive Elinor. Kate wondered bleakly why he had even bothered to come into A and E that morning to see her, speak to her, pressure her into a date that he had no real intention of keeping. Why should he want to humiliate her in such a way? Punishment because she wouldn't melt into his arms as willingly as all the others apparently did?

'I guess your friend didn't turn up,' David said quietly, some minutes later.

'No.' She mustered a smile. 'It doesn't matter. I expect he couldn't get away, after all. Doctors aren't the most reliable of men, are they?'

Her light tone convinced him that it really did not matter. He relaxed. 'Some try to be. I'd have made sure that you had a message. However, his loss is my gain.' He covered her hand lightly with his own. 'It's my lucky night. I don't usually haunt the pub, but I was hoping to see Todd Morgan. He said he'd be here about nine but there hasn't been any sign of him. Another of your unreliable doctors!'

Kate hesitated. Then she said carefully: 'He did come in. I saw him. I didn't know you wanted to see him or I'd have mentioned it at the time. He was with that staff nurse he brought to Jo's party.'

'Damn! I've missed him, then!' David frowned with a hint of annoyance.

'Something important?'

'Well, yes. It's his wallet.' He took it from his pocket. 'He left it in my office this afternoon. I'd got some tickets for the dance on Saturday and he put them in the wallet and then left it on my desk. He didn't come back so either he knows I have it and isn't worried or he can't recall what he did with it. It wouldn't matter but I'm off to Manchester for a conference first thing in the morning. I'm not due back until Friday.'

'Why not take it round to his flat? He may be there.'

'If he's with Nell then he probably won't be home until late—if he's back at all tonight.'

He spoke as though it was probable that Todd would spend the night with the staff nurse. Kate tried not to wince. 'Oh, it's *that* kind of affair,' she said airily, trying to sound like a sophisticated woman of the world instead of a very jealous girl.

'Off and on. They've known each other a long time. She goes off with someone else or he fancies another girl for a time, but they usually get together again. They'll get married one day, I daresay.'

Kate felt as though someone had squeezed her heart with a very brutal hand. She tried not to let it show. She said lightly: 'If you'll trust me with Todd's wallet, I'll see that he gets it back.' She did not know what prompted the words. The last thing she wanted was to have any further dealings with Todd Morgan!

It had already occurred to David to leave the wallet with Jimmy in Main Hall. Todd would be sure to pause briefly at the reception desk on his way to the day's work in case there might be any messages or special instructions for him. But he handed it over to Kate without hesitation. 'Good idea. I'm grateful—and I know that Todd will be, too.'

'No trouble.' Kate stowed it carefully away in her bag, refusing to admit that it was foolishly weak to want a reason for seeking him out.

'Let me get you another drink?'

She shook her head. 'I haven't the head for it. Besides, I only came in for one drink. It's been such a day and I'm dead on my feet. I'll finish this and then make a move, if you don't mind.'

He walked with her to the Nurse's Home.

'Don't forget we have a date when I get back from Manchester,' he said, reaching for her hand as they stood in the slight shelter of the doorway, out of the buffeting wind and rain.

'I'll look forward to that, David,' she said, wishing she could really mean it. He was very nice. He must be a much better recipient for her foolish heart if she was hell bent on giving it away! It would certainly be wasted on a man like Todd. But she could not feel the smallest response to his kiss and the hint of eagerness in the way he held her.

She looked after him as he walked away, tall and purposeful, an ambitious and confident man who seemed to know just where he was going in life. Kate had the conviction that she could go with him if she wished. There was something that hinted at lasting commitment in David's manner. He did not make her feel that she would be little more than a one-night stand, anyway, she thought with sudden bitterness, because that was exactly how Todd made her feel and exactly how it would be if she ever fell into the arms of such a heartless rake.

She slowly mounted the stairs to the first floor where she shared the flat with her friends. She paused in the open doorway. Jacqui's fair head was still bent over her books. Phyllida was making a hot drink with a clatter of crockery and cutlery and cupboard doors. Patti was obviously in the bath, singing at the top of her voice.

They all seemed so content with their lot that Kate was engulfed in the miserable awareness that she might never be content without Todd. Feeling that she could not bear to talk to anyone until she had conquered that choking anguish, she turned and fled.

'Left something behind . . . !' she threw over her shoulder for the benefit of her startled friends.

She emerged into the wet and chilly night, not knowing where she was going, not really caring. She walked slowly along the brightly-lit High Street towards the massive bulk of the hospital buildings, rain beating on her bare head and damping the shoulders of her coat and seeping through the thin soles of her shoes, bag tightly clenched beneath her arm.

There were lots of people about at that hour and a constant stream of passing traffic. She received one or two curious glances. Occasionally, a car slowed and the motorist hopefully sounded the horn. A man paused, seemed about to speak, but apparently thought better of it after one look at her stricken face. Kate was utterly unaware of him and everything else.

She knew it was absurd to be so disappointed in a man she had hardly known. But she had *liked* the little she had known of him, she mourned. He might not be worth a single tear, the least heartache, an atom of regret—but oh! it *hurt* that he thought so little of her that he could turn up at the Kingfisher with another girl at the very hour that they should have been meeting.

Luckily, she had only been teetering on the verge of loving him. Luckily, her heart was still her own and it would not be so very difficult to put him out of her mind and her life completely, she told herself with pride. Tomorrow . . .

Tonight, although she was hurt and angry and bewildered by his behaviour, she knew she would run into his arms if there was the smallest hope that they would close about her! So much for pride!

She was all kinds of a fool but she wanted more of those magic moments that she might never know with any other man as long as she lived. Todd was hateful, despicable, uncaring and utterly sensual and selfish—but there was enchantment in his smile, magic in his kiss, an incredible world of wonder to be found in his embrace. Her pride was swept away with the wind and the rain and she was consumed with longing. Todd owed her some kind of an explanation—and she was suddenly determined to get it even if she had to sit on his doorstep all night to see him!

Kate made her way to Clifton Street. She was not too sure of the number but she knew she would recognise the house where he lived. Reaching it, she looked up and saw the light in the top window. Her mouth was dry and her heartbeat slow and heavy, thudding against her ribs.

Todd was home, then. But was he alone—or was Elinor Nicholls with him, all warmth and invitation and yielding delight?

Briefly, Kate's courage failed. Then, prompted by anger as much as wanting, she mounted the steps and found the bell-push that bore his name. She pressed it before she could change her mind.

It was only a moment or two before she heard his voice over the intercom that controlled the opening of the door. It seemed an eternity. Her voice came out, unsteady. 'Todd? It's me—Kate . . .' She did not know what she would do if he refused to see her, she thought bleakly.

'Kate!' There was sharpness, even anger, in the swift echo of her name. 'What the devil . . .! What is it?'

Her heart sank. 'I've—something for you. Something to give you . . .' His wallet—and a piece of her mind, she thought, trying to whip up anger and only knowing that she melted inside at the mere thought of him.

Todd laughed, without humour. 'That sounds promising,' he said, mockingly. 'You'd better come up . . .'

It was neither warm nor welcoming. But it was admittance and Kate had hardly dared to expect that, in the circumstances. Having swallowed her pride so far, she did not mean to give up at this stage. She pushed open the door and began to mount the narrow staircase.

He was waiting for her at the head of the last flight, a nerve throbbing in his cheek and nothing at all to be read in his narrowed eyes. Kate saw him and checked, her heart giving a lurch and her legs turning abruptly to jelly.

She clutched at the wooden rail of the banister, wondering if she was about to faint for the first time in her life and why he should have such a violent impact on her emotions. She put a hand to her hammering heart, struggling for the breath that seemed to have been knocked right out of her body at sight of him.

'Damn these stairs!' she declared, trying to make light of that absurd reaction to a mere man and hoping he had not realised it. 'Why must you live in the clouds?'

'You must be out of condition,' he said coolly. He held out his hand. 'Come on . . .'

He drew her up the last few stairs, resisting the urge to catch her into his arms. He had been wanting her for so long that the habit might prove hard to break, he thought wryly.

Kate noticed how swiftly he dropped her hand. She glanced at him with shy uncertainty, quite unable even to say his name now that she was with him and wondering why she had come. He was so cold, so distant, so obviously uninterested. She would return his wallet and escape as quickly as she could, she decided heavily.

'You look like a drowned kitten!' he exclaimed as the light fell full on her rain-soaked face and the wet hair that clung about her small, shapely head.

'It's raining,' she said, unnecessarily. She looked towards the open door of the flat, hearing music and seeing that the lights were low, and her heart threatened to plunge to the depths. 'Is—someone with you . . . ?'

'No.'

Todd had rid himself of Elinor's company by the simple expedient of claiming to be on call. He did not really care whether or not she believed him. After all, he had found it impossible to spend the evening with her, to think of making love to her, when he was so incensed by Kate's treatment of him, so unexpected and so unjustified.

'I'm not prying,' Kate said hastily, feeling that the brusqueness of his tone was a rebuke. 'I just don't want . . . to interrupt anything,' she added, striving for lightness.

'I'm alone.'

He led the way into the sitting-room and Kate followed, looking about her and trying not to remember the last time that they had been together in his flat.

'Let me have your coat.' Todd bent down to switch on a bar of the electric fire. 'I'll make some coffee.'

'I'm not staying,' she said, quick and defensive. She did not want his reluctant hospitality and it was much too late for a show of friendliness after the earlier humiliation! Todd glanced at her with a slightly quirked eyebrow. She looked back at him as steadily as she could. 'I only came to . . . I brought your wallet.' Angry with herself for the slight stumble over the words, obvious betrayal of her nervousness, Kate fumbled in her bag.

He frowned. 'My wallet?'

'You left it in David's office.'

He stiffened at her mention of the man's name. He nodded, remembering. 'Yes. I guess I did.'

'He's going to Manchester for a few days. I expect you know. He thought he might not see you before he left. He was looking out for you in the pub tonight, actually. But you didn't stay . . .' She broke off, her voice faltering slightly. All in a rush, the feelings of that moment when she had seen him with the staff nurse came back to sweep over her.

'There didn't seem much point, you know,' he drawled. The simmering anger was threatening to boil over again as she spoke so coolly, so carelessly, of being with his friend in the Kingfisher. 'I decided it was time to stop running after a girl who doesn't want me when there are lots of girls who do.' The words were light but very cold.

The colour flew into Kate's face. 'Yes . . . well . . .' She had known how it must have been, of course. She had not expected him to be so honest. But that was Todd, she knew. She ought not to blame him for losing interest at last. Heaven knew that she had snubbed him often enough and it was the risk she had always taken. There did not seem to be anything to say in answer to that icy explanation. She held out his wallet, hand trembling almost as much as her heart. 'Anyway, David asked me to return this to you.'

His eyes narrowed. 'And you walked through this rain to do so?'

He made no move to take the wallet from her hand. Kate hesitated. Then she laid it on the low table that stood between them. 'It isn't much of a walk,' she said, very bright.

'It isn't much of a reason, either,' he said bluntly.

There was no way that she was going to give him reasons when she had no logical ones for herself. 'I didn't know when I would see you again,' she said lamely.

'You won't!'

Kate knew that he meant those quick, angry words. For whatever reason—a sudden tiring of a pursuit that seemed to get him nowhere, a sudden realisation that he preferred the other girl, anyway—he did not mean to bother with her again. If they met it would be entirely by chance. The friendship that had been so precarious and so unsatisfactory was over.

She found herself shaking, quite unable to control the reaction to the finality of his retort. She knew she should stalk out of his flat with her head high and consign him to the depths of hell with every ounce of her pride. But it took all her time to keep from hurling herself into arms that so obviously no longer wanted to hold her.

Todd thought that she shivered and he wondered what had possessed her to walk half a mile in torrential rain on such a trivial errand. After a momentary struggle with his resolution and his weakness where she was concerned, he strode into the bathroom and came out with towels.

He tossed them to her. 'Take off those wet things before you catch cold.' She looked at him, eyes widening. His mouth twisted in the travesty of a smile as he mistook her surprise for wariness. 'Oh, I won't touch you,' he assured her, mocking. 'I don't need you, Kate. There are plenty of girls in the world and most of them are willing. I've wasted too much time on you!'

The hurt welled and crashed over her like a tidal wave. She stood as if turned to stone, her teeth clamped in the soft underlip to stem the involuntary cry of protest, fighting desperately to keep back the tears that threatened to betray the shock and the pain of those scathing words.

Todd turned away and went into the kitchen without waiting to see the effect of his words, trying to tell himself that he meant them and would not weaken. He switched on the kettle and reached for the coffee jar, almost expecting to hear the slam of the flat door at any moment. Very few girls would tolerate that kind of treatment, after all.

Glancing through the open door, he saw that Kate had not moved. She clutched the towels to her breast, a stricken look in the wide grey eyes. She almost seemed to be holding her breath. His heart smote him abruptly.

He went to her and took the towels from her unresisting hands. Then he unfastened the wet coat and slid it from her shoulders. Her frock was damp to his touch, scarcely protected by the thin summer coat. The soft rose colour reflected a faint warmth into the small face. He saw that the lovely eyes were brimming with tears.

Todd hardened his heart.

Perhaps he had hurt her with the harsh words—but she had hurt him, damn it! It was too late for her to be sorry, to run after him—and he could not think of any other reason why she should make her way to his flat in such weather at an hour when junior nurses were expected to be tucked up in their beds.

She had realised that she had gone too far, of course. It had amused her to tease him, to tempt him with the sweet smile, those innocent eyes, that delicious body while keeping him at bay. She had rebuffed him continually, confident that he would be back for more—and so he had been! But she had gone too far when she decided to break their date and flaunt David's interest to make him jealous.

He had not reacted as she had expected. He had not cared—and shown it. Kate had taken sudden fright and come running, he thought grimly.

With such thoughts running through his mind and an iron control over his emotions, Todd rubbed briskly at her wet hair with a towel—and she stood like a dutiful child, allowing him to look after her. He refused to admit to a very foolish longing to take care of her for the rest of his life.

The femininity, the frailty, the air of enchanting inno-cence were all part of her undeniable appeal. This girl with her shining eyes and lovely face and shy, sweet smile could bind a man's heart with the bonds of loving, it seemed. Sir Terence, David, those other men in her life—but not himself, Todd resolved fiercely.

He gave her a little push, as if to thrust temptation away from him. 'Go and sit by the fire while I get the coffee. You look chilled to the bone!'

Kate mustered a slight smile and did as she was told, holding out cold hands to the fire. The terrible anguish about her heart had eased when Todd returned, re-moved her coat with such gentle hands and began to dry her rain-soaked hair. For he could not be so concerned if he did not care—and her heart had rallied with new hope.

Perhaps he cared more than he would admit and that might explain why he had broken their date and paraded another girl. He was proud and caring too much for any woman might humble that pride. He was sensual and he liked to feel free to take his sexual satisfaction where he could. Perhaps the sudden show of indifference had been a proud and passionate man's defence against the possibility of losing his heart and his freedom, Kate thought hopefully.

He brought her coffee and then sat down with his own, at a slight distance, regarding her thoughtfully. Kate smiled at him, a little shyly. It did not seem that he could be entirely indifferent. He sat a million miles away from her in that small room but she could almost touch the warmth of his caring, his concern, she told herself with a little lift of her heart. Relaxing, she sipped the steaming, fragrant coffee and felt its comfort steal through her slight body . . .

Todd looked at her steadily. She smiled at him over the rim of her mug like a child, a hint of shyness in the grey eyes, too pretty with the soft colour gradually stealing back into her cheeks and the rapidly-drying hair curving slightly about the small, enchanting face.

He was suddenly impatient with that pretence of shy, sweet innocence. How could she be so devious, so amoral, and remain so lovely that she could steal a man's heart before he knew it?

CHAPTER TEN

Todd fought the impulse to reach for her, enfold her in his arms. He said abruptly: 'You'll be climbing through windows again, Kate. Do you know the time?'

Kate put down her mug, very carefully. She avoided looking at him. Instead, she studied the glowing mock coals of the electric fire in the hearth. 'Couldn't I stay here . . . with you?' she said, very low. Her voice shook slightly. So did her heart. For she would not have believed it possible that she could offer herself so blatantly to any man.

Todd stiffened, stared. Then his mouth tightened and he rose to his feet. 'Don't play your tricks on me, Kate,' he said, harshly.

She understood, of course. He thought she did not mean it. He thought she meant to string him along just to disappoint him again. He did not trust her, she thought ruefully.

'It isn't a trick.' She smiled at him, rather shakily. She rose and took a step towards him and put her hand on his arm. 'I'm not very good at this kind of thing,' she said, trying to speak lightly, but in earnest. 'Throwing myself at a man, I mean. It isn't *me*. But you must know what I'm trying to say, Todd. Don't make it so hard for me!'

Todd moved from her touch, knowing what it did to his resolution. He told himself that it was easy to resist a girl who continued to lie even when there was no further need. They both knew about the other men in her life. Perhaps it was true that she did not usually need to coax a man into lovemaking. Certainly she gave herself without hesitation when it suited her, he thought bitterly. 'Why don't you know when you're not wanted?' he demanded bluntly, using her own words against her with deliberate harshness.

Kate would not allow the words to hurt. She thought of the many times that she must have hurt him and how patient he had been. Now his patience had run out and he was rejecting her in sheer self defence, she felt, not wanting to believe that he might simply have changed his mind about wanting her.

Impulsively, she put her arms about him, smiled up at him. 'I've been horrid to you. I'm sorry.' She could feel the tension and the resistance in him. 'Let me make it up to you . . .' she said softly and reached up to kiss him with shy lips.

More pretence, Todd decided angrily. He put her away from him, roughly. Then, even more roughly, he caught her back on a surge of mingled anger and passion and kissed her so fiercely that he bruised the soft mouth, held her so tightly that he crushed the tender breasts.

'Damn you!' he said, savage against her lips. 'It's time that you were taught not to play such dangerous games . . . !'

Startled, Kate found herself swept up into his arms and carried across the room and into the bedroom. He dumped her without ceremony on the wide bed and her grey eyes widened in sudden alarm.

'Todd . . . !' she warned, hands at the ready to ward him off.

He leaned over her, a glow of intent in his unsmiling eyes, and silenced her protest with his urgent mouth. His hands were urgent, too . . . at her breast and on her thighs, compelling response.

Her body quickened to his kiss, the exciting touch of his hands, the intent in this suddenly ruthless and quite determined lovemaking, even while she panicked because this was not the way it was meant to be. He was hot-blooded and quick-tempered, proud and very passionate, and it seemed that he meant to take in anger what she had refused for too long to give gladly.

Somehow, almost without her realising, he had contrived to divest her of the thin frock. But the clip of her bra briefly defeated him and she sensed the mounting impatience of his desire as he swore beneath his breath. Then he removed the flimsy garment so forcefully that he tore the material. He did not seem to notice. Surveying her nude loveliness, he caught his breath in sudden delight and, woman-like, Kate was glad that she was beautiful for him, even if her modesty was outraged and her heart thudding with apprehension.

His heart was thudding, too. She could feel it through the thin shirt as he caught her close and kissed her. Summoning all her strength, Kate pushed him away and tried to scramble from the bed. He pulled her back with angry hands and threw her down and held her captive with the weight of his hard body while he sought to kiss her again.

She jerked her head from the touch of his demanding lips. 'Don't, Todd—please, don't . . . !' she said tensely. She was beginning to be really frightened, realising how little she knew of him and knowing that he was in no mood to be gentle or kind—or deflected from taking what he wanted.

Infuriated by her resistance, Todd held her head in both strong hands and kissed her to hurt, disregarding the quiver of the soft mouth. He had expected protest, struggle, even outrage. He knew that it was all part of the pretence.

Kate wound her fingers in his dark hair and pulled, bringing his head up. 'Stop it!'

Furious, Todd wrenched her hand from his hair. 'Isn't this what you want?' he demanded roughly. 'Isn't it why you came here? Isn't it?'

'No! Yes—perhaps!' She struggled to shift his weight from her slight body. 'Not like this!' she refuted passionately. She managed to thrust him away slightly. 'Please don't do this to me, Todd,' she pleaded with a hint of desperation. 'You know I can't stop you. You're much too strong. But you can't want me to hate you!'

'I don't much care how you feel about me,' he returned without truth. 'You've been driving me mad for weeks and I'm going to have you, Kate!'

The pretence of resistance and virginal reluctance was all part of the way she liked to play it, he thought angrily, knowing how she quickened at his kiss, his touch, his urgent body against her own.

Kate was shaken by the torment in his tone. She had not realised the depths of his passion or that she excited it all the more by keeping him at bay. It had seemed to her in her innocence that a man like Todd easily overcame the desire for one woman in the arms of another. She did not know that the longing for her had been with him day and night since their first encounter.

'I didn't know . . . I didn't mean . . .' She broke off as he cupped her breast in his hand and kissed the roseate nipple with warm lips that lingered and sent swift shafting arrows of desire through her slight body. 'No!' she said forcefully. 'No!' She knew that she had to fight her own yearning even more than his passion.

Todd raised his head to look into her eyes, very tense. 'Yes,' he said, low and determined, throbbing with passion. 'You won't deny me this time, Kate . . .'

She felt all resistance ebb away as she met those compelling blue eyes and heard the urgency in his deep voice. On a sigh that was almost a sob, she put her arms about him and kissed him with warm, sweet lips in yielding surrender to the inevitable . . .

At that moment, all desire abruptly fled. On the very edge of victory, Todd knew that he would be the loser if he took advantage of that sudden surrender of lips and arms and melting body. After all, he could not take her in angry and tempestuous passion when he longed for her to lie in his arms in mutual and ecstatic loving.

Suddenly still, utterly defeated, he laid his head on her lovely breast and said, with bitterness: 'You win every time, Kate. You're too clever for me.'

Kate did not know how she had hurt him. She only knew that she had. She put her hand to his dark head and stroked the thick curls—and her heart seemed to swell with the overwhelming realisation of loving.

He had awakened her to so much more than sexual response. He had swept her into real and lasting love— and she wondered why she had not known it until that moment!

Todd tensed at the touch of her hand. Kate trembled,

wondering if he shared that incredible moment of revelation. Oh, if he loved her, too . . . ! She checked the foolish, wistful hope. She must not even dare to dream that it could be. It was enough that she loved him.

She held him, heart pounding. 'I want you,' she said, unashamedly. 'Please, Todd . . .'

He raised himself on an elbow to look at her. It was ironic that she should plead for his lovemaking when he had longed for her so often only to know disappointment, near-despair. At last he had roused her to the response he had wanted—and he could not take advantage of it!

For Todd, the sensual and careless lover of other women, found that he could not make light and meaningless love to Kate. She had become too important to him. The act of love would be too meaningful and too memorable in her arms—for him. For Kate, he might be just one more man who had fallen for the lure of her loveliness and found himself utterly bewitched. For himself—he loved her! But he did not mean to tell her so. For it seemed to Todd that the lovely Kate collected hearts without running the slightest risk of losing her own!

He drew away from those suddenly loving arms with their false promise of happiness. She tried to cling. He disengaged himself resolutely.

'Get dressed. The party's over,' he said, unsmiling.

Kate stared in dismay, disbelief. How could he sweep her to the very edge of ecstasy and then abandon her without explanation! 'Just like that . . . ?' she demanded, almost angry.

'That's right.' Todd began to button his shirt, unmoved by the look in her eyes. It was time she knew something about the frustrations she had heaped on him, he thought bitterly.

'But . . . why? I don't understand!'

'I don't care for the way you play the game,' he told her tautly. 'Perhaps you get your kicks by pushing a man to the limits of his control. I don't know. But you won't try it on me again, Kate.'

She was bewildered and shocked. He spoke as though she was sexually experienced. Is that what he thought? Didn't he know that he would have been the first if he had persisted— and that she longed with all her heart for him to be the only, the last man in her life, too? How could he look at her so, speak to her so?

'I don't know what you mean,' she said uncertainly.

His smile mocked her. 'Why don't you give up playing the innocent? We both know that you're nothing of the kind.'

She was hurt by his doubt, his contempt. She was angry, too, the colour flying in her cheeks. 'You've no reason to know any different!' she declared proudly.

'I've no reason to suppose that you're a virgin,' he returned.

There was no greater humiliation for a woman than to offer her all and be refused—unless it was to have her virginity doubted by the very man who had come nearest to taking it from her!

Kate was so furious that she flew at him, pummelled him, swore at him with words that she had not even known that she knew. Todd held her off, gripping both slender wrists with one hand, looking down at her with that hurtful mockery in his blue eyes.

'Hell hath no fury . . .' he drawled.

'It isn't that!' she raged. 'How dare you say such vile things! How dare you even think them!'

'Particularly when they happen to be true?'

At that, she wrenched a hand from his grip and slapped him with all the force of her anger and pain and hurt pride.

His eyes sparked in sudden fury. 'One day some man is going to slap you right back!' he told her angrily. 'It'll be me if you ever do that again!'

Seeing the stormy look in his eyes, she believed him. Trembling, she glowered at him. 'I hate you, Todd Morgan! I wish I'd never met you! I hope I never have to speak to you again!' Seizing her clothes, she ran from the room. Shaking all over with temper and hurt, shattered by the abrupt ending to everything between them, she scrambled into her clothes as quickly as she could.

Todd came out of the bedroom, pulling a sweater over his head. 'Ready? I'll drive you back,' he told her curtly, taking his car keys from the bureau.

'I'd rather die than put you to the trouble!' Kate thrust her arms into her damp coat, caught up her bag.

He had no intention of allowing her to walk through the streets at this hour without an escort. He cared too much to let her go as though he did not care at all.

'One favour deserves another,' he said coolly. 'You returned my wallet. The least I can do is to deliver you safely to the door on a night like this.'

'I don't want your favours!' Kate stalked to the door, head high. 'I don't want anything more to do with you at all!' She was angry enough to mean it just then.

'Then we both know where we stand.'

Her chin tilted. 'So it seems,' she said, icily, and closed the flat door behind her with a snap of finality.

Todd was at her heels before she reached the next floor, jingling his car keys as he ran lightly down the stairs behind her. Kate ignored him. As she emerged from the front door of the house, she turned resolutely in the direction of the High Street.

He caught her arm in a painful grip. 'I'll put you in the car kicking and screaming if I have to,' he warned. 'It's your choice!'

She looked at him with angry dislike. 'I wonder why I ever liked you?'

'I wonder if you ever did!'

He opened the car door. Kate hesitated. Then, thinking about that threat and suspecting that he was the kind of man to carry it out, she got in, seething.

He drove her to the Nurses' Home in a silence that neither attempted to break. Kate kept her face averted, too angry to care about the hurt that was radiating so fiercely from the region of her heart and threatening to consume her, thankful that it was only a short distance and she would soon be free for ever of the infuriating and disappointing Todd Morgan!

He drew up outside the building and turned to look at her, unsmiling. 'Do you want me to wait?' She shook her head in swift rebuttal, wanting only to be alone before the pain in her heart betrayed itself in tears. 'You might not get in,' he warned.

'That's my problem,' she said stonily.

He shrugged. 'Okay. You know where to find me if you want me.'

Meaningless words, she thought heavily. 'I won't want you!' she snapped proudly.

'Right.' He leaned across to open the car door and she flinched from the arm that lightly brushed against her breasts. 'Goodnight . . . !'

Her heart sank to the very depths. He might just as well say *goodbye*, she thought bleakly. It could not be any more final. It was foolish to expect anything else after that sudden squall. But there was no fool like a fool in love with a man who didn't want her any more! It had been a dreadful evening from beginning to end and she did not even have the comfort of knowing that it would soon be forgotten.

Todd drove off, leaving her on the pavement. Kate turned towards the door of the Nurses' Home—and then she hesitated, reluctant. She was not afraid to face Sister Vernon and she could easily invent a plausible reason for being so late. But she did not think that she could face the natural curiosity of her friends who must wonder why she had dashed off so impetuously.

She needed desperately to put some distance between herself and Hartlake, if only for a few hours. It was very late but a taxi came along just as she needed it and she hailed it thankfully, told the driver the address of her home in Hampstead and settled back on the leather seat.

Todd had drawn into the kerb a little way along the High Street, reluctant to leave her without knowing that she was all right and had gained admittance to the Nurses' Home. He watched as she ran to hail the approaching taxi. He saw her speak to the driver and climb in. A moment later, the taxi passed his parked car.

Very curious to know where she could be going at that

late hour and why she had not even attempted to get into the Nunnery, he decided to follow at a discreet distance.

It was a long way to Hampstead. Thankful that the taxi-driver had not refused the fare, Kate sat back and tried to relax and compose herself, forcing back tears, trying to put Todd and all that had happened out of her mind, happily unaware of the bronze Cortina that trailed her taxi right across London.

She paid off the taxi, tipping the driver generously. Then she searched for the key that she always carried in her purse, taking no notice at all of the car that drove up to park on the other side of the road. The house was in darkness but for the usual light in the porch. With a feeling of relief that she had gained familiar and comforting sanctuary and could cry out her heartbreak in privacy, Kate let herself in.

Todd crossed the road to look at the house, frowning. The shining brass plate beside the door caught his eye and he read the inscription without surprise. Sir Terence Murray, the neat array of initials of his medical qualifications. Dismay struck forcibly that she was on such intimate terms with the man that she possessed a key to his house and could come and go as she pleased at any hour of the day or night.

Then common-sense asserted itself. No man in the specialist's position would lay himself open to the kind of scandal that must inevitably follow an indiscreet affair with a very young girl. There had to be an explanation for Kate's easy and familiar association with Sir Terence—and Todd was rapidly beginning to realise that he had seized on the wrong one! He had been so sure that the man was Kate's lover. Now it dawned on him with a shock of dismay that he was much more likely to be an uncle or perhaps an elderly cousin. He might even be her father!

And if he had been so mistaken about the relationship that undoubtedly existed between them, then perhaps he had been wrong about everything else where Kate was concerned! Perhaps she really was the sweet and honest and entirely innocent girl that looks and manner and behaviour had led him to believe at first! Perhaps he had made the worst mistake of his life when he had come close to taking her by force that evening!

There didn't seem to be much 'perhaps' in the matter when it came to wondering if he had thrown away all his chances of happiness with the only girl he would ever love. If he was right then he certainly deserved to have lost her!

For how could he blame Kate if she refused to see or speak to him again? He had behaved quite abominably—and his attitude to her throughout had been coloured by the conviction that she and Sir Terence were lovers. It seemed almost inconceivable that he could have blundered along for so long without knowing if the name that the consultant and the junior nurse had in common was due to connection or sheer coincidence.

Kate had not talked about herself very much, he reminded himself, trying to feel a little less guilty, a little less shaken. He knew nothing about her family or her background. Their paths had crossed only now and again. He had thought that his interest in her was only sensual and maintained because she continued to keep him at a distance. He had not known until too late that it was loving as much as wanting that she stirred in him.

He tried to remember exactly what had been said whenever Sir Terence's name had cropped up in conversation—and groaned in dismay as some of his remarks came back to him. She must have known what he believed! Why hadn't she put him right? Why had she allowed him to think ill of her? Or was she so innocent that his innuendoes had gone right over that lovely head?

Todd could only be thankful that he had never actually voiced his suspicions or tackled her outright. He had not felt that he had the right to resent her relationships with other men. It was beside the point that he *had* resented them, very fiercely, angry and frustrated and jealous because she would not let him into her arms.

There had to be a reason for that, too! From the beginning, he had known that something leaped between them. Some kind of chemistry sparked desire in her as quickly as in himself. He was very sure that he could not be wrong about that! But she had held back. He had thought it a deliberate ploy to keep him in pursuit and sharpen the edge of his desire. But supposing she really was a virgin, as shy and hesitant and entirely innocent as she seemed? Then it would be very natural for her to be reluctant to become involved with a man who had his reputation for light and careless loving!

But what about David?

She had encouraged him to believe that it was a serious affair, he reminded himself defensively. He had thought that they might be lovers, although he had doubted if his friend had marriage in mind. Now, he wondered. Was any of it true? Or had she merely used David to deter him from chasing her?

Were they lovers, in fact? To Todd, that was the all-important question.

For if Kate was a virgin, then his behaviour had been utterly unforgivable and he might as well give up all hope of winning her.

But if she was not, then she should be able to understand that his need of her had overcome all other considerations—and she must have known just what she was doing when she held out her arms to him so unexpectedly!

CHAPTER ELEVEN

KATE went down to breakfast, heavy-eyed after a virtually sleepless night and heavy-hearted because there was no future in loving Todd and she knew that she would go on loving him, wanting him.

She explained to her surprised parents that she had stayed late at a friend's flat and then lacked the courage to rouse Home Sister at dead of night. Instead, she had impulsively hailed a taxi and come home.

Remembering her own training at Hartlake and quite forgetting that the present Home Sister was not the rigid and old-fashioned disciplinarian who had terrified all the juniors in her day, Judith Murray quite understood. Sir Terence regarded his wan daughter with a very thoughtful look in his eyes and said little.

As it happened, he was due at Hartlake that morning to consult with Sir Lionel Fielding, the surgeon who was to remove the diseased gall-bladder of one of his patients . . . and Kate was not due on duty until one o'clock that day. She would be back at Hartlake in plenty of time to explain and apologise to Sister Vernon and receive the expected scold before she changed into uniform for work on A and E.

Having parked his car in its reserved bay behind the hospital, Sir Terence walked with his daughter across the garden and they entered the main building through the swing doors. He was on his way to his office and Kate was taking the short cut to the High Street and the

Nurses' Home. The tall, silver-haired consultant was a very distinguished and well-known figure. Few people realised that the slender girl in the elegant tailored suit who walked with him was the blonde junior from A and E.

Todd was in Main Hall, talking to Jimmy, the head porter. And he was making a point of talking about Sir Terence just as the man himself came into view, turning to speak to his companion with a smile that held something in it of Kate's own sweet, swift smile.

'Father and daughter,' Todd said, quite involuntarily—and it was not a question. All the dismay of the previous night when he had stood outside that house in Hampstead came crashing down on him again. If she ever realised just what he had suspected . . . ! Todd almost groaned aloud.

Jimmy followed his gaze, grinned. 'Now I'm not saying anything, Dr Morgan. Gave my word I wouldn't. I don't know how these things get around, but I'm not responsible for grapevine gossip, you know . . .'

Todd scarcely heard. His heart was thudding. Would she notice him? Would she look through him with chips of ice where the lovely eyes should be? Would she realise just how much he regretted what had happened and how much he cared and grant him just a glimpse of her smile? Either way, he had to know what she was thinking and feeling about him this morning!

He moved purposefully towards her as she stood with Sir Terence, waiting for the descending lift . . .

'Come and have a cup of coffee,' Sir Terence suggested, glancing at his watch. 'We've plenty of time and I want to talk to you.'

Kate was suddenly wary, knowing that particular note in his voice. 'Haven't we been talking all the way here?' she returned lightly, defensively.

'Skating over surfaces,' he said dryly.

They were very close. She had confided in him all her life, bringing her troubles and problems to him, seeking his advice. He knew now that there was something on her mind. He suspected that there was only one thing she would not confide to him—a love affair that was going wrong.

Sir Terence was very concerned for his daughter. She was very young and she had always wanted to nurse. It would be a pity if some man made her so unhappy that she decided to give up her training. But at that age hearts were very vulnerable and a disappointment could seem the end of the world.

'Something's troubling you, Kate—and that troubles me,' he said gently. 'What is it? Changed your mind about nursing?'

'Oh no!'

That was emphatic enough, anyway, he decided. 'What brought you rushing home in the middle of the night? Why do you look so washed out this morning? I don't think you're sleeping, Kate. I'll try a snap diagnosis. I think you've caught a bug that often attacks the young, mostly in spring. Known to the layman as love,' he said, eyes twinkling. 'Fortunately it isn't fatal. But it can be uncomfortable while it lasts.'

Kate was suddenly close to tears. She didn't want kindness, sympathy, understanding—and, least of all, advice, even from a loving father who cared about her happiness. She just wanted to be left alone to cope with her feelings and try to overcome them. For it wasn't a scrap of good caring for a man like Todd!

It was at that moment that Todd reached them, more attractive than ever and as confident of a welcome as if she did not have every reason to detest and despise him, Kate thought resentfully, ignoring him and the somersault of her heart.

He nodded to her father. 'Good morning, sir.' It was the courteous, deferential greeting of a junior doctor to a senior and respected member of the same profession. Outwardly cool and confident, he looked at Kate's lovely and expressionless face with a sinking heart.

Sir Terence was not a man to stand on his dignity. He smiled pleasantly. 'How are you . . . ?'

'Morgan, sir,' Todd supplied promptly. 'Sir Lionel's houseman . . .'

'Ah, yes . . .' Sir Terence waited until the lift emptied and ushered his daughter inside, followed by the tall young man whose eyes were so intent on Kate's lovely face. She carefully avoided looking at him. Sensing the charged atmosphere, Sir Terence looked at the young doctor with new interest. Morgan, eh? He must sound out Lionel Fielding on his houseman's character and background and career potential, he decided.

Kate was young but, like her mother, she was quick to know her own mind and slow to change it. He saw that her face was no longer too pale but suffused with delicate colour. There was a familiar hint of obstinacy in the set of her sweet mouth. He recalled another girl, even lovelier than Kate to his eyes, who had fallen headlong in love at Hartlake and had been too stubborn to admit it until it was almost too late.

'I daresay you know my daughter, Dr Morgan,' he said, a little dryly, as the lift doors slid across—and felt the pinch of Kate's fingers in swift and furious reproach.

'Oh, we're old friends,' Todd said lightly, outrageously. 'Aren't we, Kate?' For all the lightness of words and smile, there was a very definite plea for forgiveness and understanding in the blue eyes.

She looked at him then, with daggers. 'Weren't we?' she agreed, very sweetly, ice tinkling. The lift halted at the first floor and she turned to her father. Todd was waiting courteously for them to precede him from the lift, holding the doors open with a finger on the button. 'I've changed my mind about that coffee,' she said brightly. 'I really think I ought to see Home Sister as soon as possible.'

Sir Terence was not deceived by the light tone or her smile. He understood that she abruptly needed to escape from a young man that she obviously knew too well. 'All right, darling,' he agreed. 'I shall be about the hospital for most of the morning. I'll try to see you before I leave.'

He walked from the lift. Kate expected that Todd would follow. He did not. Disconcerted, she glanced at him as the doors slid shut, cutting her father from view. Now, they were the only occupants of the lift, usually so crowded. He could not have planned it that way, of course. But it was like him to take swift advantage of it—and she wondered that he could be so unrepentant, so unashamed, so very sure of himself in the circumstances!

Todd's hand hovered by the lift-buttons. 'Up or down?' he asked coolly, knowing perfectly well.

She hated him for forcing her to speak. She was hot all over, remembering—and knowing it would be impossible ever to forget. Equally impossible ever to forgive him, too! 'Down,' she said stiffly. 'Ground floor . . .'

He nodded, pressed the button. 'Your father is an attractive man,' he said idly. She said nothing. 'You aren't at all like him.'

She knew he was being deliberately provocative but she was still goaded into retort. 'Thanks!'

A smile flickered. 'I expect you resemble your mother,' he said gently. 'I believe that she's a very beautiful woman.' She was silent. She did not mean to make it easy for him, he thought ruefully—and tried a different tack. 'Did you have trouble last night? I heard you mention Home Sister. On the carpet, are you?'

'I don't wish to talk about last night,' she said, coldly, chin tilting.

He hesitated. Then he said quietly: 'I made every mistake in the book, didn't I, Kate? I don't expect you to forgive me . . .'

'Very sensible. I won't!' she snapped.

Kate walked out of the lift and he followed. She ignored him. He fell into step by her side as she hurried across Main Hall, not even turning her head to smile as usual when Jimmy called a friendly greeting.

The big man looked after the couple with a knowing expression in his eyes. He had seen it all before—more times than he could count!

Todd held open the main door to the street and Kate sailed through, head high. He hurried after her, caught her arm. She wrenched it away.

'Kate!' he said, urgently.

'Leave me alone, Todd,' she warned, very near to exploding or bursting into tears at his persistence. What did he want? What did he hope to gain? Didn't he know that it was all over and that it was impossible to pick up the shattered pieces?

'We have to talk,' he told her firmly, barring her way as she tried to walk on. 'Not here and now, perhaps. But soon!'

'We've nothing to say to each other!'

People looked at them curiously, the tall and very good-looking doctor with the stethoscope dangling from the pocket of his white coat and the slender, fair girl who did not seem to care if the whole world knew that she was angry.

Conscious of the glances and the interest they were attracting, Todd drew her slightly to one side, away from the stream of people on their way in or out of the hospital. It was the merest touch of his hand on her arm, removed before she could resent it.

'You must know how sorry I am,' he said quietly. 'Do you want me to grovel?' There was the hint of a wry smile in the blue eyes.

'I want you to get out of my life so I can forget that I ever knew you!' Kate tried to mean the furious words. But the touch of his hand had unsteadied her heart and almost undermined the pride that would not allow any man to get away with the way he had treated her.

His eyes darkened, narrowed. He had expected lingering anger, resentment, distrust. It shook him to realise that it might well be loathing that shone from those lovely eyes and echoed in the violent words of rejection. 'Do you hate me that much?' he demanded, needing to know what he was battling against.

Kate's heart swelled. 'Yes, I do!' she declared, defiant.

The fool! The stupid, insensitive idiot! Didn't he realise that love, not hate, had taken her to his flat despite the conviction that he cared nothing at all for her? If she hated him as she ought would she have cared what he did or what he was? Would she have hurled herself at him? Would she be so hurt, so angry, so determined to safeguard herself against loving him even more?

Pride almost spun him on his heel and sent him off to the ward where he had been due for rounds ten minutes before. Love and need kept him looking into the stormy eyes, searching desperately for the smallest sign that might allow him to hope even if he had to wait to be forgiven.

'I don't want to lose you,' he said, bluntly. It seemed to be the only thing he could say. It was certainly not the moment to tell her that he loved her, he thought wryly. She would not believe him. She would not even listen in her present mood.

Kate drew in her breath sharply. Did he think she could forgive and forget so easily? Did he think she was used to being insulted and assaulted and very nearly raped by men who never once allowed the word *love* to fall from their lips? Did he think she would throw her arms about him then and there and admit that she didn't want to lose him either? Just like that? How little he knew her!

'You never had me,' she reminded him, tartly. 'You never will!'

He looked down at her steadily. 'Never is a long time, Kate,' he said quietly. 'But I'll wait.'

He meant it. For the first time, he loved as he had never expected to love any woman . . . deeply and irrevocably and with marriage in mind. He wanted to marry her and keep her close, cherish her and make her happy, know the many joys that she could bring him—until the end of time!

Kate almost ran from the look in his blue eyes, not daring to believe it. He would only hurt and disappoint her again! Strange, unpredictable and unfathomable man who would not give up the pursuit even when he must know that he could not win!

Perhaps he had forgotten the insults he had thrown at her. Perhaps he could dismiss that near-rape as a mere bagatelle, a silly woman's fuss about nothing. Perhaps the chase and the conquest was everything and he did not give a damn for the consequences.

It was entirely different to Kate, still outraged. She might have been able to forgive him if she was not burning with the humiliation of having already ceded victory—and knowing that he had chosen not to take it . . .

Working on Accident and Emergency, she felt reasonably safe from chance encounters with a doctor who ought to be busy about his own work on the wards. And if he came looking for her she would complain to Sister Carmichael and he would certainly get a reprimand from his boss. Then he might accept that she really did not want to have anything further to do with him.

So Kate was not too pleased to be transferred to a ward only the next day—and when she discovered that Todd was in and out of Paterson throughout the day, she almost wondered if even Matron had succumbed to his charm and his fatal fascination. She would not have been at all surprised to learn that Todd had arranged things so that their paths should cross frequently!

But she soon found that he took very little notice of her on the ward. Either he was being unusually discreet or he was much too busy or he was heeding her angry words—or he had abruptly lost all interest in that careless and quite unpredictable way that he had!

I don't want to lose you, he had said. But it seemed that he was not making the slightest attempt to win back her liking and friendship. Kate was too proud and too stubborn to show that it mattered in the slightest.

Paterson was a women's surgical ward and she quickly adapted to the difference in the day's work. She had enjoyed A and E, but it had been demanding and it was something of a relief to work on a ward that did not deal almost exclusively with tragedies and disasters. It was a busy ward and some of the patients were very ill. But a high percentage of them got well and went home. Kate liked the opportunity to know the patients as people instead of just names. There was time to put faces to the names, to learn about husbands and children, to feel personally involved with the women who found her a sympathetic listener and confided some of their anxieties along with their symptoms.

Kate found the routine of rounds relaxing after the hectic pace of A and E, too. Sister Hamilton was good-natured and cheerful and very easy-going for all the brisk efficiency with which the ward was run.

It was a happy ward and that was good for the morale of the patients. Kate was moved by the courage and the concern for others that some of them displayed, coming in for major surgery and dreading it, but able to laugh and make jokes and rally other patients and even flirt with the doctors, managing to put on a brave and cheerful face for visitors along with the indispensable lipstick and pretty nightdress or bedjacket.

Todd was very popular with the patients and on excellent terms with Sister and the rest of the ward staff. Most of the juniors sighed over him and talked about him at length and did their best to attract his interest— and it sometimes seemed to Kate that she heard the name of Todd Morgan morning, noon and night. She did her best not to sigh over him and tried not to listen to gossip about his many light-hearted affairs and resolutely behaved as though he did not exist except as just another doctor about the ward—and she was thankful that she was much too junior to have to work with him. At the same time, she was learning more about him every day—and liking what she saw and heard.

He spent much of his day on Paterson and the adjoining men's ward, Currie. He was concerned with the preoperative and postoperative treatment of patients admitted by his boss, Sir Lionel Fielding. He examined each new patient on admission, took copious notes, ordered X-rays and medication, explained the proposed surgery and soothed fears and anxieties about the after-effects, discussed care and diet and prognosis with ward staff.

He did the early morning round with Sister or the

senior staff nurse and a much longer round later in th
day with Sir Lionel or one of his registrars, accompanie
by a group of students if it happened to be a teachin
round.

He took blood samples, set up drips, inserted o
replaced vital tubes before and after surgery, checke
lab reports and talked to relatives. He attended Si
Lionel's clinic twice a week. He observed and assisted a
operations and checked the postoperative condition o
patients and followed their progress until discharge—o
death as happened in some cases, for all their combine
efforts.

He was on call for most of the day and sometimes a
night. In his little free time, he was working for hi
FRCS.

He was working too hard, Kate felt, anxious eyes
observing the signs of strain and the deepening lines o
tension in his attractive face. He did not seem to smile s
readily any more and the juniors were commenting or
his failure to talk and laugh and flirt with them and the
patients in his former endearing manner.

At times, he looked so tired and so down at the end of
a long day that Kate ached to draw his dark head to her
breast and give him some relief and some release from
tension in her arms. But she was careful not to show her
concern and compassion—and she was much too proud
and much too stubborn to admit her caring.

For since that day on the hospital steps, not a word
had passed between them that the whole world might
not have overheard. His smile was superficial. His touch
was impersonal and usually accidental. His interest
appeared to be non-existent these days.

Loving him, the need and the longing grew stronger with every passing day and the hope that things would eventually come right between them grew weaker. For he did not seem to want her, after all . . .

Todd was waiting for her to make the first move. He was sure that Kate knew just how he felt about her. Women were supposed to have an unfailing instinct in such matters and he had made no secret of his love or his need. He had not hesitated to humble his pride for the sake of the girl he loved.

But he was prepared for a very long wait. Kate's eyes were cool and guarded whenever they met his own, on or off the ward. Her smiles were meaningless, if she smiled at him at all. She spoke to him only if it was unavoidable. She hurried into sluice or kitchen or juniors' room if she saw him coming along a corridor—and she avoided him in club or pub or at the parties that he went to only because he knew that she had been invited. He came away hurt and resentful and almost despairing because the lovely Kate had bestowed her sweet smile, the warmth of her liking, the generosity of her friendship on apparently every man but himself.

Patience had never been Todd's strong suit. Celibacy was hard for a man with his sensual nature. But he loved Kate. So he had to wait until she was prepared to relent and give him another chance—and it would never happen at all if she thought he was in hot pursuit of other girls.

There were pretty girls in plenty. Some were very willing to give him what Kate would not—friendship, affection, sexual satisfaction. Not one of them stirred his senses or his heart.

He only wanted Kate.

He refused to believe that David was a threat to all his hopes despite the friendship between the registrar and Kate that was rapidly turning into courtship if the grapevine was to be believed. But the anxiety in him deepened every time that he saw them together . . . and that was much too often!

Some of Professor Wilmot's patients were admitted to Paterson, too. As his senior registrar, David was a frequent visitor to the ward. Senior doctors did not usually break all the traditional rules of etiquette by chatting up junior nurses and David was more discreet than most in that respect. But he did manage the occasional word with Kate and they met regularly when both were off duty.

In fact, they were friends. Kate liked him and had become fond of him. He was an attractive escort and excellent company—and he knew just how to treat a woman, she thought defiantly, refusing to remember that even Todd's cavalier attitude to all women had not prevented her from falling deeply in love with him.

She went to dances and parties and other places with David—and wondered if it was only chance that Todd seemed to be in so many of those places at the same time. His failure to approach her or to whisk her out of David's arms seemed to prove that it was certainly not by design.

Todd seemed to have turned into a loner. He did not arrive at pub or club or party with any particular girl and Kate noticed that he did not leave with any of the girls who hung about him. He flirted, but that was second nature to a man like Todd. It did not seem to mean very much. She wondered about Elinor Nicholls and was relieved to learn that she was now going around with one of the lab technicians . . . until she recalled David's remarks about the on-off affair that would probably end in marriage between Todd and the staff nurse.

Kate did not care for the thought that the strain and tension, the seeming depression and the odd lack of interest in women that Todd was showing so plainly might be due to the loss of Elinor rather than herself.

I don't want to lose you, he had said.

Kate wished with all her heart that he had meant the obviously empty words . . .

CHAPTER TWELVE

TODD's year of 'walking the wards' was almost over and he had applied for a registrar's post on another surgical firm. He wanted to specialise in renal surgery eventually and that was the next step on the ladder of his ambition.

He was delighted to learn that he had been accepted. It meant that Sir Lionel Fielding had given him an excellent reference and that his work in the year since he had qualified had been generally satisfactory. He had worked very hard to that end and it was good to know that it had paid off.

Professionally, he was content with the way things were going for him. His personal life had gone badly amiss.

Daily, he grew more anxious about Kate. Happiness with her was even more important than his career and the hope of it never left him. The likelihood of sharing the rest of his life with her seemed to become more remote with every new dawn.

Had he been too patient? He had waited and watched and said nothing while her relationship with David grew into a very real threat. Suddenly it occurred to him that Kate might suppose he did not care because he did not act!

Faint heart never won fair lady. The old saying leapt to his mind. In the past, he had reached out and taken any girl he wanted with smiling self-assurance. But he

162

had been faint-hearted, utterly unsure, when it came to Kate. Falling so unexpectedly in love, he had been out of his depth from the very beginning. He had blundered badly and things had gone steadily from bad to worse until now it seemed only too probable that he had lost the only lady he would ever love.

For years, he had been ending affairs with girls who found it too easy to love him while he was not ready for that kind of commitment. Suddenly and irrevocably committed before he knew what was happening to his heart, Todd simply did not know how to go about persuading Kate to love him. Everything he did and said seemed to be wrong.

But loving her was *right*—his destiny! It was a very firm conviction . . . and he could not be moved from another and equally firm conviction that they were meant to be together until the end of time, David or no David!

On his way to the ward with the letter of appointment tucked securely into his wallet, Todd paused by the door of the sterilising-room at sight of the girl he recognised with his heart before his eyes registered that slender figure in the neat and pretty uniform that suited her so well.

She was busy at the autoclave, taking out the gleaming instruments and placing them carefully in a sterile dish.

Todd stepped into the room. 'Kate . . .' he said with sudden longing.

She had been intent on what she was doing and the need to ensure that no instrument touched an unsterile surface. For once, she had not been thinking about Todd—and she was so startled by the unexpected sound of his voice and that urgency in the way he said her name that she dropped a pair of forceps to the floor. 'What do you want?' she exclaimed, annoyed with herself for that sudden, betraying start—and her clumsiness.

'Sorry about that,' he said wryly. He stooped to retrieve the forceps and dropped them in a tray that held instruments waiting to go into the autoclave. 'I seem to spend my life apologising to you, Kate. I wonder why.'

'Could it be because you're thoughtless, irresponsible and utterly unreliable?' she suggested sweetly.

Todd winced at the words, but it was encouraging that she was actually talking to him after days of behaving as though he did not exist.

He smiled at her as though her retort had not hurt him. 'I'm glad my boss doesn't share your view of me—and that I didn't have to rely on you for a reference. I might not have got the job I was after!'

Kate glanced at him, heart lurching with a little dismay. She did not want him to leave Hartlake and go out of her life for ever! She had known that his appointment as houseman to Sir Lionel was coming to an end. She remembered that he had spoken about going into general practice. It seemed that his plans to do so could easily take him to any part of the country—and she might never see him again!

'Tell me about it,' she invited, careful to convey only polite interest. 'Is it a good job?'

'Assistant registrar in renal surgery. It's what I want. With any luck, I might get to be a consultant after a few years in the field.' The euphoria he had felt on learning of the appointment was deflated by her obvious indifference. For what was there to work for if he did not have

Kate by his side to encourage him, to applaud his successes and sympathise with his setbacks, to help him achieve his ambition by ensuring his peace of mind and his heart's content?

Kate knew that luck played very little part in achieving such an ambition. It took hard work and dedication and genuine caring as well as skill and that extra special something that made a capable surgeon recognised as a brilliant one.

She did not doubt that Todd would get what he wanted. There was purpose and strength of mind and a certain integrity about him that she could not help admiring, even when she was most angry with him. Her heart was suddenly heavy at the thought that she would never share in his success and his satisfaction.

'Well, I'm very pleased for you,' she said, coolly because the warmth of loving threatened to overwhelm her and she had no reason to believe that it would be welcome. 'I hope everything works out for you, Todd.'

The days had passed without any sign that she cared because they were no longer friends who might have become lasting lovers. Now she wished him well without warmth. Any man would be discouraged. But Todd still carried that inner conviction that it would all come right eventually if he was only patient and loved her enough.

'Everything will,' he said confidently. 'I'm sure of it!'

'When do you leave us?' Hartlake and herself, Kate meant.

'End of June,' he returned, meaning Paterson.

The Renal Unit was in another wing of the hospital. He wondered wryly how much he would see of Kate once he took up the new appointment. Working on the same ward had meant almost daily contact with her, however unsatisfactory.

Too soon, she thought with dread.

'Oh, ages yet,' she said as though it really mattered very little. She began to put away the sterile instruments.

Todd had a very busy day before him, as usual. Sister Hamilton must be waiting for him to do the round. He did not have the time to stand and watch while a junior nurse did the work that was part of the daily routine of the ward, but he could not tear himself away.

'How do you like it on the ward after A and E?' he asked lightly.

'Very much. A and E was exciting. But I like to have time to talk to the patients. One feels more involved.'

He nodded. 'They like you, Kate.'

'Do they?' She glanced at him, gratified.

'I've heard some very nice things about you,' he said. He smiled with sudden warmth. 'Nothing that I didn't already know for myself, of course.'

A little colour stole into her face at the implied compliment. Her foolish heart turned over at the devastating impact of his smile. 'The patients like you, too,' she said carefully. 'You'll be very much missed.' By me more than anyone, she thought bleakly.

By those who don't really matter, he thought heavily. 'Oh, I don't know,' he demurred. 'One doctor is much like another where patients are concerned. They don't care who makes them well as long as someone does. That's just how it should be.'

'It's important that they feel a doctor really cares— and you do!' Kate said quickly. 'You're concerned and compassionate and genuinely interested in them as people—and it shows. I think you're a very good doctor!'

'I didn't think you'd noticed,' he said quizzically.

'I can't help knowing what people feel about you,' she said defensively. 'You're very popular.'

'Except with you.'

She was very intent on peeling off the thin surgical gloves with which she had handled the instruments. 'You lose a lot of sleep over that,' she said, mocking, thinking bitterly how little he had tried to mend matters and how unlikely it was that he cared if she liked him or not.

The words flicked him on the raw. He had spent too many nights thinking of her, longing for her—and dreaming about her when he did finally get to sleep.

'More than you know,' he said, quickly, angrily. 'Damn you, Kate! Do you think I don't care? Do you think I—'

'There you are, Nurse!' Sister interrupted the hot words with a hint of impatience and a frown of disapproval for the junior who was wasting time in flirting with the very attractive houseman who was known to flirt with too many girls. 'Haven't you finished yet? It's time for rounds!'

'Yes, Sister. Sorry, Sister,' Kate said, automatically. Her eyes were held by Todd's intent and angry gaze and her heart was much too busy wondering what he had been on the point of saying to care for Sister's annoyance.

'Then go and help Nurse Young, please—at once!'

'Yes, Sister . . .' Kate knew better than to disobey. But she went unwillingly.

Sister Hamilton looked after the reluctant girl as she hurried along the corridor to the ward. 'You have a gift for distracting my juniors from their work,' she said dryly, without censure. She was no more immune to Todd Morgan's good looks and undeniable charm than her juniors and found she could forgive him a great deal.

'And you have a gift for interrupting at the wrong moment,' he retorted with the acceptable frankness of friendship. They had known each other since he was a medical student and she was a third-year nurse. 'It's taken me days to get near that girl!'

'Sorry,' she said blithely. 'But I daresay that charm of yours will have its usual effect in the end. I'd be grateful if you'd refrain from exercising it on my ward!'

They strolled into the ward to begin the round in perfect amity. Todd looked instinctively for Kate as he always did these days. She was going from bed to bed, inserting thermometers in the mouths of patients, her sweet smile accompanying the routine task.

Sweet and lovely Kate. He could not lose her to David or any other man. Somehow he had to make sure of his happiness before it was too late. Surely there was some small spark that could be fanned into renewed flame—if only he could find the right words, the right way!

The round, briefer than usual, seemed endless. Todd was much too conscious of Kate, her slim figure passing by too often as she went about her work, checking pulses and reading thermometers and entering details on each patient's chart.

It was difficult for him to concentrate on his own work as he stood by a bed, talking and smiling and reassuring, reading the chart to check the progress or deterioration of the patient's condition, listening to what Sister or the patient had to tell him and deciding on further treatment or discharge. His head and his heart were full of Kate. His eyes strayed too often to the fair head, bent over a patient.

Kate was conscious of him, too. She knew that he turned to watch her as she went up or down the ward, attending to patients. She tried not to meet the blue eyes that tilted her heart with their enchantment. She tried not to think of the touch of his hand or the way he had kissed and held her. It made the ache for him so much fiercer. It made her feel like rushing across the ward and throwing her arms about him in defiance of etiquette and Sister! It made her love him too much and wish with all her heart that he loved her, too.

Do you think I don't care?

The words echoed, filling her with hope. If only Sister hadn't come in at just that moment, scolding and sending her back to the ward. She might have found that Todd did care, wanted her still, and that the heartache of recent days could be forgotten and forgiven in his arms.

Pulse and temps round over, Kate hung about the corridor in the hope of seeing Todd. He was so busy that he might only have time for a brief word. But it might be the one word that she desperately wanted to hear, she thought, heart lifting, remembering the way that he had once called her *darling* and touched her cheek. At the time she had thought so little of the warmth in his eyes and voice. Now, the memory haunted her continually. Perhaps it had meant nothing. Perhaps it had meant everything that a woman could want . . .

Todd came out of the ward, thrusting his way through

the swing doors, white coat flying in the draught. He was immediately followed by Sister Hamilton who had paused only briefly to give an instruction to her senior staff nurse.

Kate vanished into the sluice at sight of the ward sister and busied herself with the pile of waiting bedpans.

But there had been a moment when she and Todd had looked at each other and there had been a hint of a smile in his blue eyes. For the first time in days, she felt that loving him might not be such a disaster, after all . . .

Todd accompanied Sister Hamilton into her office where they discussed the condition of a patient who was not doing as well as she should after an operation to remove an obstruction in the bile duct. The jaundice was clearing satisfactorily but she had developed respiratory problems and would need careful nursing for a few days.

He doodled absently on a notepad close to his hand on the desk while they talked. 'I don't like the look of her,' he said at length. 'I think we'll put her in a side ward.'

Sister Hamilton disagreed. Women liked the company of other patients and the cheerful bustle of the big wards. Mrs Wells was a nervous patient and would probably be unnecessarily alarmed by the move. So many of the patients associated the small side wards with the seriously ill and dying—and, of course, it was true that such patients were nursed away from the main ward whenever possible.

'She came in convinced that she had cancer. She's just beginning to accept that a rather large gallstone was the villain of the piece, after all. If we move her into a side ward at this point, she'll get frightened all over again. We know that she's going to be all right once we clear the chest infection. She doesn't,' she said firmly.

Todd nodded. 'Okay. We'll leave her where she is and see how she does.' He threw down the pen, rose. 'I must be on my way. Nothing else, is there?'

'No time for tea?'

'Not this morning . . .'

He smiled at her and left—and Sister Hamilton thought to herself that his smile reminded her of the Cheshire Cat in *Alice*. It seemed to linger after he had gone, warming her and brightening the most difficult of days. He would be much missed when he joined the Renal Unit.

She reached for the pad with its neat list of reminders—and raised an eyebrow as she realised that it had been almost obliterated. Dr Morgan's mind had obviously been far from Mrs Wells and her chest infection, she thought dryly.

While they talked, he had doodled and the page was scrawled with a name that had been ornamented and embellished in a variety of ways. The same name over and over again . . . *Kate*. There were drawings, too. One of a girl in the unmistakable frock of a Hartlake nurse with a tiny cap perched on her head. Another of a very similar girl in bridal gown and veil. He had considerable talent and he had captured the likeness of her newest junior extremely well.

Sister Hamilton smiled. It was easy to know what had been in his mind, she thought, amused and just a little surprised. She had not supposed that Todd Morgan was the marrying kind!

Kate came out of the sluice just as Todd left Sister's office and walked briskly along the corridor in her direction. He looked so preoccupied that she hesitated to approach him. She did not know what to say to him, anyway. But words were not always necessary. Sometimes a look or a smile could speak volumes. So she looked at him and smiled, a little shyly.

Encouraged by that unexpected smile, Todd came to an abrupt halt. He looked down at the delicately lovely face that dominated his dreams, waking and sleeping. Almost, he kissed her then and there at that long-awaited hint of forgiveness.

Instead, he said brusquely: 'Founder's Ball on Saturday. Like to come with me, Kate?' He had not meant to hurl it at her head as though he didn't much care whether she came or not, he thought wryly, and wondered why he went to pieces whenever he looked into the wide grey eyes that seemed to mirror the sweetness and the innocence and the integrity of this girl.

Kate bit her lip. He had left it just too late, she thought unhappily. Only last night, she had finally agreed that David should be her escort, having left her answer as long as she decently could in the seemingly vain hope that Todd would make her first Founder's Ball a memorable one for her by asking her to go with him. For many Hartlake nurses through the years, such an invitation had been a sure sign of serious interest and the promise of a lasting and worthwhile relationship.

Now, her heart didn't know whether to soar in delight at the invitation or plunge in dismay because she had to refuse it.

'I can't . . .' she said unevenly, fighting bitter disappointment and the temptation to abandon all her principles and disappoint David!

His eyes narrowed. 'Does that mean *won't*?' he demanded bluntly.

'I'm going with David.' Kate saw the sensual mouth tighten abruptly and saw the betraying nerve begin to jump in the lean cheek. She had not meant to sound defiant. He probably thought it was one more snub to add to all the others. 'I'm sorry, Todd,' she said quickly.

He looked at her with hard and angry eyes. 'I doubt it.'

'Why didn't you ask me yesterday?' she said impulsively, almost accusing.

He raised an eyebrow. 'Would it have made a difference?' His tone mocked her mock regret.

'I only said yes to David last night!' she told him truthfully.

'I daresay you say yes to David in all things these days,' he said deliberately.

The colour surged into her small face. 'You are mistaken,' she said, low.

'I hope I am!'

Her chin went up at that. 'Why? Because he mustn't have what you didn't want?' She threw the words at him, hurt and resentment flooding back because he could think ill of her so readily.

'You know damn well how much I wanted you—and a lot of good it did me!' he said angrily.

'You turned me down!' She was too hot with anger to check the passionate and impulsive words.

He frowned. 'Is that what rankles?' he asked swiftly. 'I had my reasons, Kate!'

'Well, if one of them was revenge it must have given you a great deal of satisfaction,' she told him bitterly.

He looked down at her ruefully. 'If that's what you think then we are a million miles away from being friends.'

She could never be content with friendship, Kate thought heavily. She wanted his love. If she could not have that then she wanted nothing at all from the man who would soon be going out of her life for good.

'We'll never be friends . . .' Her voice trembled. 'Never!'

'I'm beginning to believe it,' he said heavily. He put a hand on her shoulder, gripping hard. 'You're always with David these days. Are you in love with him?'

His fingers were bruising. She would be black and blue! But her heart lifted at the savage intensity of his tone. *Do you think I don't care . . . ?* Suddenly she knew that he did. But he had hurt her and humiliated her— and she was not yet ready to forgive and forget.

'I don't see why I should answer that question,' she said coolly. 'You've absolutely no right to ask it!'

Todd was heartened by the evasion. Kate was not the kind of girl to keep a man dangling on a string, he felt. She must know that he loved her with all his heart. If it was hopeless, she would say so. Her failure to say so made him suddenly sure that he had been right to go on hoping all these weeks.

He bent his dark head, purposefully. Kate tried to evade the touch of his lips, tried to wriggle from the firm clasp of his hand on her shoulder. But he kissed her, hard—and in full view of an elderly patient in a dressing-gown on her way to the day room and a couple of wardmaids who were watching with avid interest from the kitchen. Kate could only be thankful that Sister had not seen and sent her smartly to Matron for breaking one of the strictest of hospital rules.

Todd sensed the brief quickening and melting of her lips beneath his own, and the response she could not help or disguise was all the answer that he had needed.

'Now tell me that I haven't the right to kiss you, either,' he said lightly. His hand moved from her shoulder to the nape of her neck and rested there in a brief caress. He smiled down at her with the warmth and enchantment that few women had ever been able to resist.

Kate filled with love for him—and she might have blurted it out then and there if his personal radio had not interrupted the tense moment.

Saved by the 'bleep', she thought as he reluctantly left her and hurried to the nearest telephone. The moment was lost, but her heart was singing as she went back to the ward and her work.

For surely there would be another time when both moment and mood were right . . .

CHAPTER THIRTEEN

KATE knew she ought to be annoyed with Todd for kissing her in the ward corridor, exposing her to the risk of instant dismissal. Nurses and doctors weren't supposed to behave like ordinary human beings when they were in uniform and on duty.

Certainly he shouldn't have invited the gossip that was already going the rounds on the ward and off it. But his smile, his touch, the look in his eyes—all memories that she continually hugged to her heart during the day—made it quite impossible for her to be cross with him.

In fact, she was walking on air, suddenly the happiest girl at Hartlake, in love and daring to dream that she was loved.

She sang in the sluice and almost waltzed about the ward, eyes bright and cheeks flushed and heart lifting at the thought of the happiness to come.

Several patients smiled at her and at each other, for she was young and rather sweet and genuinely interested in them as people as well as cases—and some of them sighed, remembering days when they had been young and in love and filled with hope for the future . . .

Being a sentimental and warm-hearted girl, Sister Hamilton smiled, too—and thought of the way that Todd Morgan had drawn pictures of the junior nurse all over her notepad. She had to pretend to know nothing of that kiss in the corridor, of course. It would be a pity to scold the girl whose eyes were shining with dreams of happy-ever-after!

But wasn't that just like devil-may-care Todd to snatch a kiss because he wanted it and to hell with surroundings or consequences or anything else? She sighed a little sigh because he had never even thought of snatching a kiss from her and, like too many girls, she had always liked him too much for comfort . . .

The other nurses teased Kate about that kiss. The story, recounted and exaggerated by the two ward-maids, lost nothing in the telling as it spread like a forest fire throughout Hartlake by virtue of the ever-efficient grapevine.

Kate laughed and blushed and shook her head to all the probing questions—and blushed even deeper when Todd walked unexpectedly into the kitchen in the middle of it all.

'Is it a private party or can anyone join in?' he asked, very dry. The lack of a smile in eyes or voice stilled the laughter in a moment. 'Sorry to spoil your fun, but there's riot and rumpus on the ward. Mrs Blair has fallen out of bed again and Mrs Sinclair is being sick and there's two admissions on their way from A and E . . .'

Everyone fled except Kate who went on with her task of making up a milk feed for a patient on special diet, hoping devoutly that he had not heard any of the ribald remarks that had brought such warmth to her face.

'What was all that about?' he asked quietly.

'Nothing much,' she returned lightly.

'Congratulating you, were they?'

Struck by something in his tone, Kate glanced at him swiftly. Her heart sank at the expression in his eyes.

'I believe we're engaged,' he went on coolly. 'It's all over the hospital.'

Her eyes widened. 'But that's ridiculous!' she exclaimed, annoyed with the gossips who had spread such an absurdity on the strength of one kiss.

'Isn't it?' he drawled.

Her heart lurched suddenly. 'You don't think *I've* been saying so, surely!' she demanded indignantly, chin shooting up in swift pride. Did he think that she was trying to trap him into an engagement, for heaven's sake? He was stiff, disapproving, slightly angry. Was he so sure that every girl must want to marry him? The conceit of the man! It was Kate's dearest wish, her heart's desire—but nothing on earth would make her admit it now!

'Well, *I* haven't.'

'Of course not! Why should you? Everyone knows that you aren't the marrying kind,' she returned, tartly. 'Bed them not wed them—isn't that your motto?' Furiously, she whisked the milk drink into a frothy mix.

A smile flickered at that show of spirit. He had been annoyed by the rumour, by the sly glances, by the back-thumping of his friends who pretended to believe that he had been caught at last—and it had been the last straw when a very youthful junior had burst into tears because he meant to marry another girl. Now, he thought that it did not matter what the grapevine said or thought. All that really mattered was Kate's reaction to the idea of marrying him.

'So far,' he agreed smoothly. 'If and when I change my mind and ask a girl to marry me, I shall want a little time to get used to the idea before the whole world knows about it.'

Kate bridled instinctively at that 'if and when' with all its careless arrogance. 'Whatever makes you think that any girl would want to marry you?' she demanded hotly. 'For my part, I'd rather marry Dracula!'

Todd smiled at her with sudden warmth. 'I should wait until you're asked before you start throwing refusals in my face,' he said lightly.

'Don't ask,' she advised, very sweetly. 'A slapped face sometimes offends.' She stalked from the kitchen with the feeding cup.

Arrogant, infuriating devil! How dare he be so sure of himself—so infuriatingly sure of her! How dare he smile at her in the way that tumbled her heart—and know it!

Trembling, she spilled some of the feed on the patient's sheets. She was not thinking very kindly of Todd as she came out of the linen cupboard with a plastic pack of clean sheets for the bed. He was standing by the swing doors of the ward, talking to David.

David moved swiftly to open the door for her with his usual courtesy. She thanked him with one of her warmest smiles. She sailed past Todd as though he simply did not exist—and spoiled the effect by glancing back to see if it had bothered him. His eyes crinkled with warm laughter. He was very attractive, very endearing—and Kate hurried to her work before her foolish heart betrayed how much he meant to her.

Half an hour later, she went off duty—and looked in vain for Todd before she left the ward. She was one of the fortunates who had the next day off and would have plenty of time to get ready for Founder's Ball. Knowing that Todd would be working all day, Kate thought it only too likely that they would not meet until then—and she would be with David. It hurt to think that Todd would probably be with some other girl.

She looked for him on her way to Main Hall. His name strip was missing from the indicator board behind Jimmy. He had gone off duty, too.

'Looking forward to the Ball, Nurse?' Jimmy hailed her cheerfully. 'I expect you're going with one of your boy-friends. Hard to choose between them, I daresay. Your mum used to have the same problem. Had 'em all running round in circles, she did!'

Kate smiled at the big man. She doubted if he remembered her mother out of all the many nurses who had trained at Hartlake through the years. But he liked to pretend that he did. 'I'm going with Mr Montgomery.' It was no secret. Just as well if she didn't want the entire hospital to know, she thought dryly, convinced that much of the grapevine gossip began with the romantic old man.

'Are you now? I wonder why I thought you'd be going with Dr Morgan,' he said slyly.

'I was too far back in the queue,' she returned lightly. 'But I expect you know who *is* going with him!'

Jimmy grinned. 'Got a way with the girls, that one,' he declared warmly. 'But he'll meet his match—if he hasn't already! I've seen worse than him turn into respectable married men—and it doesn't hurt as much as they think it will, as I always tell 'em!'

Kate laughed, aware that her strategy had failed. If Jimmy did know that Todd had quickly found himself another partner, he was not telling. 'Marriage is going out of fashion,' she said lightly. 'Didn't you know?'

'Never!' he said stoutly. 'Not in my lifetime—or beyond it! It's a great institution.'

'I didn't know you were married,' she teased, playing up to him, knowing that Hartlake had always been his whole life.

'Oh, I'm not, love. Never could abide institutions,' he said, grinning.

Kate gave a mock groan at the corny old gag and left him. Walking along the High Street to the Nurses' Home, she half-expected Todd to appear at her side at any moment. She was disappointed.

He was so unpredictable, she thought wryly. Perhaps that was part of his charm. But she wanted very much to see him, to be with him—and she felt very let down after the earlier promise in the way he had kissed her. Had it meant nothing at all? Was that why he had been so cross because it had been exaggerated out of all proportion by the gossips?

Remembering the look in his eyes, the warmth of his lips, Kate was tempted to believe that it had meant all she could wish . . . love and longing and lasting commitment.

But hadn't there been an awful lot of girls in Todd's life who had foolishly believed just the same thing . . . ?

Kate took special pains with face and hair and clothes for the evening with David. Founder's Ball was a gala occasion. She had promised to go with David and it was impossible for her to let him down. But she wished with all her heart that it could be Todd for whom she put on the swirling chiffon frock of coral pink that exactly matched the shade of her lipstick and brushed her pale hair until it shone and curved prettily about her face.

She knew that she looked her very best. All that was missing was a certain glow that only Todd could bring to the eyes that mirrored the state of her heart. This evening, it was fretting for the man she loved, would always love.

The feet that would have danced all the way to meet Todd dragged a little as she went down to the wide hall in response to the message that her escort had arrived. It was not fair to David to be so reluctant, she knew. But she could not help it. The evening that might be so magical and so memorable if only she could spend it with Todd seemed to hold very little promise of delight with David. Nice though he was, much as she liked him, he did not stir her senses and touch her heart and fill her with dreaming.

'You look lovely,' he told her warmly, tucking her hand possessively into his arm as they walked through the throng towards the table close to the dance floor where some of their friends were already gathered. 'The belle of the ball!'

Kate smiled up at him with affection, tightened her hand on his arm. He was a dear—and really very dear to her. But he was not Todd . . . and she looked eagerly for him in the crowded ballroom that throbbed with music and conversation and laughter.

Nurses were dressed in their prettiest finery or, due to go on duty or having just come from the wards, looked distinctive in the traditional uniform and caps. Many of the younger doctors had discarded inhibition with their white coats for the evening and were intent on enjoying the occasion and the pretty girls.

The atmosphere was infectious. Convinced that she could not enjoy the Ball without Todd, it was still possible to find some pleasure in the music and the dancing, the company of friends, the flattering attention of David and other men who came crowding about her in eager admiration. Kate talked and smiled and danced and gave a fairly convincing display of enjoyment. But her heart was longing for Todd to arrive—as someone had carelessly assured her that he would when he was ready in reply to an equally careless query.

In that whirling throng, it was hard to distinguish one man from another. Several times, she thought she saw Todd on the dance floor. Anxious scrutiny proved that it wasn't Todd at all and she could relax until the next time—but she was beginning to wonder if she would see him at all that evening. For it was getting late and there was no sign of him. Perhaps he had decided to stay away—or perhaps he was enjoying himself in a very different way in very different company, she thought bleakly.

At last, he came. Making his way towards the group of tables which had been pushed together at the edge of the dance floor and where she sat with David and the others. Tall and handsome and very distinctive—and unmistakably Todd! Kate's heart missed a beat.

He was wearing a formal dinner jacket of midnight blue and a dress shirt of powder blue, open at the neck to reveal a heavy gold chain. Lean and bronzed and masculine and very sure of himself, he was much too attractive, Kate thought wryly, noting how many heads turned, how many girls smiled at him with warm invitation—and how readily he smiled back, paused to speak, put a careless arm about a slender waist or a pair of bare shoulders. Attractive and popular and very much a man, he looked and behaved like the Casanova that she knew him to be—and Kate wondered if loving him was likely to bring her any happiness at all.

A woman would never know where she was with Todd Morgan. He was too fickle, too sensual, too unreliable. Worst of all, he seemed to be entirely heart-whole. She was a fool to suppose that his desire for her owed anything to loving. Why on earth had she lost her heart to him when it would have been so much safer in David's reliable and considerate keeping—or her own!

As he drew near, his glance sought and found Kate and she saw the quickening of appreciation and admiration in his blue eyes. A smile trembled on her lips, betraying her delight for all her proud resolution. A hand fluttered as if tempted to reach out to him in eager greeting and then flew to her breast to still the suddenly hammering heart.

Smiling, very sure of his welcome, Todd joined the lively party. After a warm exchange of greetings and compliments, he turned to where Kate sat with David's arm about her waist.

'Kate . . .' he said warmly, turning her name into an unmistakable and very tender endearment. He laid a hand on her slight shoulder and bent to kiss her lips with the easy assurance of the lover, his mouth lingering just long enough to tell the world how he felt about her.

The small and very lovely face was a study of mingled outrage and delight, suffused with warm colour, as he straightened.

The men cheered. The girls smiled and pretended that

they were not envious of that direct and entirely typical declaration of interest and intent.

David smiled, too. But he was not amused. It was not the fact that Todd had kissed her in full view of everyone that disturbed him so much. It was just the kind of thing that Todd would do! It was the look in Kate's eyes, the quiver of involuntary response to that kiss, that told David that the growing hope of a meaningful and long-lasting relationship with the lovely girl had been nipped neatly in the bud by his friend.

He wished he knew what it was about Todd that made too many girls fall headlong in love with him. He wished that Kate had not made the same mistake. Then, looking at Todd, he wondered if it was a mistake, after all. For there was a certain glow in his friend's eyes as he smiled at Kate that he had never seen there before.

David stifled a sigh of resignation. Kate was not the first girl he had lost to Todd Morgan. It did seem that she might well be the last . . .

Kate, conscious of so many amused and interested eyes upon her, wished she could sink through the floor. She did not know whether to hurl something at Todd's head or throw her arms about him. He could not have chosen a more public place to single her out as an object of his interest, she thought crossly. It was just a game to him, a delight in giving people something to talk about, a careless lack of concern for convention or anything else!

As he straightened, smiling, much too sure that she had wanted and welcomed his kiss, Kate looked away from the compelling blue eyes and the smile that had swept her into loving. She ought to be able to laugh, to scold him lightly, to turn the whole thing into an amusing joke for the benefit of watching friends. She could not.

With all her heart, she wanted to believe that his kiss had been a promise of real happiness and not just a tantalising tease. But how could any girl be sure of anything with a man like Todd!

She stared at the dance floor but the sea of moving couples were just a blur for the tears that filled her eyes. The sound of the music was a muffled background to the echo of his deep voice saying her name. Her heart was beating so high and so hard in her throat that she wondered if she was going to faint.

Todd had expected some reaction but she neither smiled nor spoke. Nor did she meet his eyes after that first startled glance. He waited—and she turned her head to look at the dancers, ignoring him.

The snub hit him like a blow. He loved her and he had told her and the whole world so in the way he kissed her, said her name. She had shown him and the whole world that she did not want his love. Todd was suddenly pale beneath the deep tan of his handsome face. His eyes darkened and a nerve began to throb in the lean cheek.

About to turn away, to accept defeat at last, he saw the betraying quiver of her sweet mouth, the hint of tears on those incredibly long and unexpectedly dark lashes. His heart stirred and hope renewed itself.

As if they were the only two people in that crowded ballroom, he reached for her hand. She turned a startled face to him. 'Dance with me, Kate,' he said and it was command rather than suggestion.

Her heart fluttered. He smiled into her eyes so warmly, with such tenderness, that she fell a little deeper into love in that moment. Her heart steadied and filled with delight. For surely there was all that any woman could want in that smile—and surely there could be no more doubt or dismay, mistakes or misunderstandings, if he really cared.

Without looking to David to see if he minded, Kate rose and walked to the dance floor with Todd and slipped into his waiting arms as if she belonged in them for the rest of her life. She knew she did not want to be in any other man's arms for as long as she lived—and Todd's embrace held a great deal of warm and satisfying reassurance as he drew her close.

They moved to the music without speaking, needing those few moments of nearness. She liked the strength of his arms about her and she thrilled to the movement of his hard body against her own. This man stirred heart, soul and body with his magic and she loved him very much. She hoped that he loved her . . .

Dancing with her gave Todd the excuse he needed to hold her but it was a torment. The lovely body against his own evoked swift, fierce desire. He loved her so much. He wanted her desperately. He hoped with all his heart that she would agree to marry him.

He pressed his lips to the pale, shining halo of her hair. 'Darling . . .' he said softly, achingly. He felt her slight involuntary response to the endearment and was heartened. His arms about her became even more of an embrace. 'I used to know all the words, all the ways, to get what I wanted when a girl didn't matter too much. Now, I'm lost.' He sighed, lips close to her soft cheek, his warm breath ruffling the soft strands of her hair. 'Kate, you matter such a lot. Tell me what I need to say or do!'

A dream suddenly seemed very near to its fulfilment. Kate looked at him, smiling. 'I don't know what it is you want, Todd,' she demurred gently.

'I want to marry you,' he said simply, without pride, without passion. 'I love you.'

Her heart soared with thankfulness at those words from a man whose integrity would surely never allow him to say what wasn't true and meant. 'Oh, Todd,' she said with a wealth of love and longing in her voice, in the way she touched her hand to his lean, loved face. 'What other words do you need . . . ?'

And she reached to put both arms about his neck and kissed him in warm and melting surrender—and a murmur of delight rippled through the ballroom as Hartlake recognised that yet another romance between a doctor and a pretty nurse was on the way to a happy ending.

Two more Doctor Nurse Romances to look out for this month

Mills & Boon Doctor Nurse Romances are proving very popular indeed. Stories range wide throughout the world of medicine – from high-technology modern hospitals to the lonely life of a nurse in a small rural community.

These are the other two titles for July.

NURSE FOSTER
by Rhona Uren

When Ward Sister Zena Foster falls in love with one of her patients, a wealthy young Arab businessman, she decides to work in a hospital in Kuwait for a year before making up her mind to accept his marriage proposal. But the attractive neuro-surgeon, Theodore Smythe, seems determined to thwart her plans . . .

DAMSEL IN GREEN
by Betty Neels

After Nurse Georgina Rodman has nursed two children in Casualty, their guardian, Professor van den Berg Eyffert, arranges for her to continue to look after them during their convalescence. For some reason it is not long before Georgina finds herself wishing she could be with them – and their guardian – 'for keeps'.

On sale where you buy Mills & Boon romances

The Mills & Boon rose is the rose of romance

Look out for these three great Doctor Nurse Romances coming next month

DR HARTNELL'S DISCOVERY
by Elizabeth Petty

While out riding, Sister Lara Groves rescues a man who has been badly injured in a fall from his horse. But when he turns out to be the new consultant at the hospital where she works, it seems that that chance meeting will lead to nothing but heartache.

TALISMAN FOR A SURGEON
by Lisa Cooper

Sister Rosalind Mason feels upset and humiliated after her rows with the suave, elegant and eminent surgeon, Peregrine Bradford. But as a friend warns her, hatred is akin to love . . .

THE PURSUIT OF DR LLOYD
by Marjorie Norrell

When Dr Michael Lloyd comes to St Jude's, more than one nurse is intrigued. But is Staff Nurse Elizabeth Fletcher being really honest when she says she is more interested in him as a doctor than as a romantic possibility?

On sale where you buy Mills & Boon romances.

The Mills & Boon rose is the rose of romance

ROMANCE

Variety is the spice of romance

Each month, Mills & Boon publish new romances. New stories about people falling in love. A world of variety in romance – from the best writers in the romantic world. Choose from these titles in July.

FORGOTTEN LOVER Carole Mortimer
LATE HARVEST Yvonne Whittal
STARTING OVER Lynsey Stevens
BROKEN RHAPSODY Margaret Way
BLIND MAN'S BUFF Victoria Gordon
LESSON IN LOVE Claudia Jameson
MIDNIGHT LOVER Charlotte Lamb
STORM CYCLE Margaret Pargeter
PACIFIC PRETENCE Daphne Clair
WILDFIRE ENCOUNTER Helen Bianchin
THE OTHER BROTHER Jessica Steele
THE MAGNOLIA SIEGE Pamela Pope

On sale where you buy paperbacks. If you require further information or have any difficulty obtaining them, write to: Mills & Boon Reader Service, PO Box 236, Thornton Road, Croydon, Surrey CR9 3RU, England.

Mills & Boon
the rose of romance